Pax Vobis Jack
by
Viv Seaman

Pax Vobis Jack
by Viv Seaman

Copyright © 2010 Viv Seaman

Published by
PB Software
3 Nelson Road
Ashingdon, Rochford
Essex SS4 3EJ

FIRST EDITION
First Printing January 2011

A CIP catalogue record of this book
is available from the British Library

ISBN 978-0-9565891-7-0

Cover by: Jennifer Shaw

After many years as a primary school teacher, Viv Seaman turned to writing. She has published several humorous articles and had her short story, 'Message From Mel', included in Richard and Judy's 'Winning Stories,' a collection for children.

For my wonderful

grandchildren,

Hannah, Thomas,

Olivia and Lucy

CHAPTER 1

"Gotcha, teacher's pet!"

Jack yelped and grabbed his leg as blood seeped through his trousers.

Zak Dreyfus smirked, waving the geometry compass mockingly.

"Oh dear! Hurt, did it?"

The year seven kids were noisy as they queued in the corridor outside the classroom. Jack didn't cry but if he had, no-one would have noticed.

The door opened.

"OK," the teacher called. "Come in." In the rush, no-one saw Josh Smith's heavy shoe smash against Jack's shin.

"Settle down Year seven."

Mrs. Hunter slammed the pile of exercise books on to her desk and scowled at the class.

"I WILL teach you tearaways to value your history if it kills me! Roman pedagogues didn't have this trouble with their pupils."

She picked up the first book and glanced at it.

"Josh Smith, catch!" She sent the scruffy exercise book flying through the air to land with a 'plonk' on Josh's desk.

"Rubbish! Untidy. Not thought out and in the main, the facts are wrong. Do it again."

Josh shrugged.

"Like I care!" he muttered under his breath.

Mrs. Hunter continued with her book-throwing skills until half-way down the pile.

"I don't know why I bother!" She grumbled, scooping up the rest and dumping them in front of a boy who was fiddling with a Blackberry.

"Do something for once, Zak Dreyfus, give these out. It's probably the most useful thing you'll achieve in my lesson anyway."

Mrs. Hunter had kept back one book. She opened it and scanned the pages.

"Well done Jack. A brilliant essay and nicely presented. It's good to know that at least one of my pupils has a grasp on the fantastic world of history. I feel as if I'm actually in Rome when I read your work."

Jack Page cringed, wishing he'd put in less effort but he couldn't help it. When he wrote about ancient Rome he almost felt he could be there. It fascinated him. Next time he wouldn't be so clever.

Mrs. Hunter turned to write on the board.

"I've got eyes in the back of my head Zak. Put that blackberry away and get on. Right you can all have a go at this, even you young ladies! Imagine you're a slave or a servant. Write what you feel."

There was a general hum of giggling, mainly from the girls. Mrs. Hunter was famed for her sarcasm.

"OK. Any offers for ideas for the opening sentence?"

The teacher scanned the room for a response.

"You, you and you put your hands down." She was looking for someone who hadn't volunteered.

"No, not you either my little Einstein of the history world," she said, addressing Jack. "I think we'll ask Josh to have a go. You're a young lad washing the wounds of war from a soldier's body. So, what do we write now?"

Josh wriggled in his seat."

"Well?"

Josh shrugged.

"OK. Tell him Einstein."

Jack pretended he hadn't heard.

"Come on Jack," Mrs. Hunter cajoled, holding the piece of chalk in his direction.

Slowly, Jack got to his feet and shuffled down to the front of the class. He felt small beside Josh Smith and his mate Zak Dreyfus. They'd get him for this. There'd be nowhere to hide. They'd get their own back. Quickly, Jack scrawled on the board.

"My master bleeds from the cuts of the sword. I wash him."

"See! It's not gobble-de-gook. It is do-able. Well done, Jack." Mrs. Hunter was making things worse.

Jack scuttled back to his place, keeping his eyes to the ground. Looking up, he caught Zenith's sympathetic glance. He nodded at her.

The lesson continued but Jack's concentration was interrupted by his mobile phone vibrating in his blazer pocket. It was his Dad's old phone and he'd only got it when Dad needed a more updated one for the business. It was very old-fashioned and Jack had taken a lot of stick about it. All it was good for was calls and texts. One day, if his dad's business did OK, he'd ask for a really good one. One you could take pictures with. He'd seen one in a shop that had a built-in camcorder. They wouldn't laugh at him then.

Glancing around, Jack slipped the mobile out of his pocket and held it below desk level. There was a text. '*U.R. dead teachers pet corridors R 4 killing.*' It was the third text like that he'd had since yesterday. He knew he shouldn't read them but how could he not?

Jack felt sick.

When the bell went he didn't know what to do. He just knew he couldn't tell anyone. Not about the threats, not about being stabbed with the compass, not about anything. He knew better than to tell.

"OK. Year Seven. It's literacy. Don't linger in the corridor. Get along to your next lesson." Mrs. Hunter's voice followed them down the corridor as the class scrambled out.

Zenith caught up with Jack.

"D'you think they'll have another go?" She asked.

Jack frowned.

"What d'you mean?" She was much taller than him so he had to look up to speak to her.

"The bullies. I know about them. And I saw your face when you looked at your mobile."

"How? I haven't told anyone. How do you know?"

"Don't look so scared. I'm on your side. You're not the only one getting it."

"Zak and Josh are thumping you around too? A girl?"

"No not them. Some of the girls. The ones in their gang."

"Why?" Zenith was ordinary and Josh couldn't see anything to bully her for, except she was quite pretty. Maybe they were jealous."

"My name. That's why."

"Oh." It was difficult to say anything else. Jack didn't want to be disloyal. After all she was being friendly but it was an odd name.

"It means highest point or place of greatest power or happiness. My parents are ambitious for me. I wish I was called Emma or something ordinary, like everyone else. Come on, we'll be late. See you after literacy."

He'd seen Josh Smith and Zak Dreyfus coming along the corridor so he tried to think of something else to say. They probably wouldn't do anything while he was talking to someone but she ran off towards the next class. As he neared the English room, Josh and Zak jumped him, dragging him along the floor of the corridor so his elbows scraped the ground.

"Shall we kill him now?" Zak threatened in a smarmy tone, bearing down on him from a height and landing one booted kick in his side. Jack, winded and in pain, let out a howl.

"Teacher! Scarper!"

It was Josh's voice. They dropped their hold on him and ran. The teacher frowned down at Jack.

"Name?

"Jack Page, Sir." He scrambled to his feet.

"Year?"

"Year seven."

"So what happened?"

"Don't know, Sir."

"What d'you mean, you don't know? Well?"

Jack said nothing. He just stood there shivering. He knew better than to name names. That would get him into far worse trouble than he was already. If the teacher hauled Josh and Zak out they would know he'd snitched. Better to play dumb. The teacher spoke again.

"We don't have bullying at this school. If you've been bullied you need to tell someone. OK?"

Jack nodded.

"Well?" Jack remained silent. He couldn't say anything. He just couldn't. The teacher became impatient.

"Well I can't help you if you don't help me. What lesson

are you supposed to be in next?"

"Literacy, Sir."

"With?"

"Mrs. Philmore."

"Well, get along there now." The teacher stopped at the door and turned back towards Jack.

"And if you remember their names come and find me in the staff-room."

Jack belted back to the classroom, just making the end of the queue as the lesson bell rang. He slunk into the only vacant seat in the front row noticing Josh, Zak and the rest of their gang already seated at the back. He shoved his P.E. Kit and his back pack under the desk. After a while he heard sniggering but it didn't last long. Mrs. Philmore was strict.

"Clauses," she said as if it was a swear word, "and commas."

Her voice droned on but Jack was lost in thought. Somehow he had to avoid them. He had no idea why they picked on him. He hadn't given them any cause. He hadn't reported them. He just wanted to be left alone. He couldn't help it if he liked history.

"Jack Page, wake up and take an active part in this lesson. You haven't been listening to a word I've said and it's only Monday. You've got the rest of the week to get through yet."

Jack stared at the teacher and said,

"Yes Miss." He had other things on his mind. It wasn't just the bullying. It was the awful weekend. Seeing his mum again had been great. But staying in her new house with her new husband Ben, had been odd. Uncomfortable. Like he didn't really belong.

"Jack, I won't tell you again." The teacher's voice cut into his thoughts and Jack nodded and picked up his pencil in the hopes that his brain would work.

"Psst!"

Jack looked round.

"Psst!"

It was Zenith trying to get his attention. She was mouthing something at him but he couldn't make out what. Simultaneously they checked on Mrs. Philmore but she was still writing on the board and had her back to them.

"They've got it. Your bag, they've got it." Zenith whispered, inclining her head towards the back of the room where Zak, Josh and a couple of others were playing around with something under the desks.

Jack bent down to feel for his bag. It wasn't there. He turned as he heard shuffling behind him. Movement at the back of the room caught his eye. Jack stared, disbelievingly. Josh and Zak were playing footie under the desks, with his bag. Josh looked him straight in the eye and smirked.

"So what're you going to do about it?" the look said. Jack turned away and stared at his desk. He could hear his bag slithering around the floor.

"What is that noise?" Mrs. Philmore, sounded exasperated.

"It's Jack's bag," giggled Ellie, one of the girls in Josh's gang. "It's slipping about all over the place." The class sniggered

"Go and pick it up Jack." Mrs. Philmore kept her cool. "And don't bring it into class in future."

Jack shuffled to the back and rescued his bag. He kept his head down to avoid everyone's eyes. He hated being the centre of attention. How was he supposed to avoid bringing his stuff into school, when his mother planned to drop him off at school every Monday morning after the weekend visits?

The lesson dragged on and Mrs. Philmore found other people to pick on.

After school, Jack headed for home. It wasn't very far. His father would still be working and the van with the words on it, 'J. Page, Carpenter. All wood-work undertaken,' would not be on the front drive until Dad had finished work for the night. Jack had a key and usually got home before his father.

He kicked a discarded coke can along the pavement dribbling, then aiming it hard into a kerb-side 'goal-mouth'.

"Yeah!" It was a precision kick. It hit the exact spot he had aimed at.

He was quite used to going home alone now and getting himself a snack and watching TV. Sometimes he'd kick a ball around in the back garden until his father came home. What he was not allowed to do was go off anywhere else, not with his friends or anything else until his father returned and could know exactly where Jack intended to be. He was nearly home now and was just deciding whether to watch TV or have a session on the computer after he got in, when he doubled over in pain, winded.

Someone had his neck in an arm-lock. A fist punched his stomach. He felt the straps of his back-pack being dragged from his grasp.

"Gotcha Einstein! Ah! Poor little Einstein, thinks he's cleverer than everyone else."

Zak was making fun of Jack while punching the daylights out of him. Jack hit the ground with his elbow and yelled in pain. He hurt everywhere.

"Look what I've got!" Zak let go of Jack as Josh held up Jack's back pack.

Josh drop kicked the bag into the mud.

"What d'yer think of that then, teacher's pet?" He crowed.

Zak dribbled the bag in the mud then kicked it back to Josh, who lobbed it high into the air and into the path of a car, which squashed the bag into the mud.

Zak laughed, as he and Josh ran off giggling leaving Jack sat sprawled in the mud. The bag lay open, pyjamas and underwear spilling out on to the road. Jack got to his feet somehow. His clothes were filthy and his left arm was agony. He waited until the road was clear, then limped out and stuffed his belongings back into his bag with one arm and hobbled off.

"I hate Ben. It's all his fault," he said.

Realising that he had spoken his thoughts about his step-father out loud, he glanced around to make sure no-one was near enough to hear him. They'd say he was a loony.

"If it wasn't for Ben, Mum and Dad would still be married and I wouldn't need a flipping weekend bag," he muttered.

Jack shook his head. What was he going to do now? If he walked towards his house, the other two might be lying in wait for him. They had gone off in that direction.

Jack turned back the other way towards the cliffs. He sat on one of the wooden seats that nestled among the neat rose beds on the well-kept grass verges.

"What am I going to do now?" he whispered to himself. Jack looked out across the waters of the mouth of the Thames that stretched from Essex to Kent.

A party of seagulls were bobbing about on the surface in the distance. They didn't look real from up there. To his right, to the west, the industrial chimneys of Canvey Island puffed out steam. Across the water, there were chimneys too, of the power stations but also fields that seemed to run right down into the water on the other side. Jack caught the strong smell of seaweed wafting in with the tide.

An area of land much nearer to him drew his attention, probably because the gulls, had swooped up into the air and glided to Two Tree Island. Jack had been there of course, hundreds of times with his dad. Well a few anyway. It was good for bird-watching and there was a golf range. And a council dump where Dad took the garden rubbish.

Jack clambered down the steep stone steps to the bottom of the cliffs. He made his way to the narrow road that ran alongside Leigh train station and formed a bridge to the nearly deserted island.

The rough ground in the distance that served as a car park was almost empty of cars. It ran down to the water inlet where hundreds of different species of birds bobbed about on the surface or nested in the near-by greenery or hopped tamely near the parked vehicles.

Jack clutched his bag tightly as he trudged along the tarmac path, his footsteps getting slower and slower. He felt exhausted and his arm ached. How could he go home now when Zak or Josh were lying in wait ready to pounce out at him and start hitting him about again? What on earth was he going to do?

Feet dragging, Jack headed for the far side of the car park where the sea just lapped the tarmac. An old lump of wood, once a break-water but now gnarled and decaying, protruded from the seaweed-slimy froth at the water's edge. The smell of the seaweed was strong that afternoon. Jack dropped his bag on dry ground and slumped down on the wood in relief as if his tired legs could stand up no longer. He licked his lips and tasted salt left there by the chill afternoon wind.

"NO-----OH!" He yelled. "It's not fair! Why do they always pick on me?" His frustration overcoming him at last, he let out a piercing scream but there was no-one to help him and his voice was carried out to sea. Finally, because there was no-one, he let the tears of misery run down his face.

He kicked angrily at the oozing, froth-covered mud at the water's edge. Something beneath his foot caught the light and he bent to pick it up. It was a scruffy old coin, too dirt covered for Jack to make out its value.

His thoughts were racing. He couldn't stand any more bullying.

"I'd rather be dead," he hiccoughed between sobs at a gull that had perched one-legged, on another breakwater just near him. Still holding the coin, he clenched his good fist in misery and in anger.

What could he do?

He stood up, facing out to sea. He was mesmerised by the roll and swish of the water. The water! It looked so inviting, so comforting. He walked beyond the water's edge so the froth oozed over his toecaps. Further he walked and further until water swirled around his ankles, his knees, his thighs. It was cold. He didn't care any more. There was nobody here to bully him.

The icy water reached his waist. Then his neck.

Forcing his body against the strength of the water, he continued walking.

CHAPTER 2

Jack coughed and spluttered and heaved up a huge amount of mucky, green seawater. He hurt everywhere. His legs, his left arm especially and his throbbing head. His lungs felt as if they were going to explode. He was spread-eagled on the ground. He tried to sit up and focus his eyes. Water trickled down his face, so that he could only just make out the misty shape of a boy bending over him.

"Salutations," the boy said.

Jack stared up at him.

"Who are you?"

"Greetings." The boy's words were strange.

"What's your name? Why are you dressed like a girl?" Jack barked rudely, suddenly fully awake.

In front of him stood a boy about his own age. A boy in a white dress. For a split second, Jack tried to laugh but it hurt too much. Huh! If the bullies made fun of him, what would they do to a boy wearing a girl's dress? He looked him up and down. And open-toed sandals?

"You are new here. I do not recognise you."

The boy's matter-of-fact statement annoyed Jack. He was in no mood to be bullied any more.

"I've been here loads of times. With my dad mainly," he snapped. "You're the new one."

"You were under the water. I thought you were dead."

Jack gave the boy an odd look before glancing down at himself. Slowly it dawned on him his clothes were dripping wet.

The two boys eyed each other and there was an uneasy silence. Then they both spoke together.

"I pulled you out of the sea. Your body and clothes were very heavy with water. Why were you there? What happened?"

"Why are you dressed like a girl?" Jack repeated, answering the stranger's question with one of his own but his impolite inquiry remained unanswered by the strange boy.

"What were you doing in the water when you could easily have drowned?" the stranger went on, "For if I hadn't been there to pull you out you would indeed have been taken by the waves."

Jack shrugged his shoulders and thought hard before answering.

"I couldn't go on. I wanted to die."

"You tried to drown yourself? That is very cowardly! You entered the water in order to die?" By his shocked tone of voice it was obvious that the boy was disgusted.

"You don't understand," Jack whispered, "I've been bullied and bullied and bullied 'til I'm sick of it. They pick on me for everything. They pick on me just for breathing. I couldn't stand any more."

"That is no excuse. When boys hurt me, I must be brave. I must fight back. It is the Roman way. I should not like to be branded a coward."

Jack was incensed. What did this boy know?

"I bet you've never been picked on," he shouted now. "It bloody hurts. Anyway, what's your name?" Jack asked again, determined to get the upper hand. He was not going to let anyone else kick him around like Zak or Josh had. Then he said,

"Just don't mess me around, OK? I've had enough of it."

The boy took no notice of his unfriendly tone.

"You should thank me for saving your life. You do not have good manners. And I am not dressed like a girl. I am wearing the tunic of course because I am not yet old enough to wear the full toga." It was the boy's turn to snap a response. " Every intelligent person knows that."

Painfully, Jack struggled to his feet still intent on snubbing him.

"Toga?" Jack knew full well what a toga was but it just didn't make sense. Not on Two Tree Island in the twenty-first century.

"Yes. One day my family will return to Rome. The toga is a sign of Roman citizenship. Our great senators wear togas with a purple edge. A mark of importance. I shall not be a senator. I shall be a great warrior. I shall be a centurion like my grandfather."

Completely baffled by the strange words, Jack thought the boy seemed so sure of himself that he couldn't help being impressed and decided to be friendly. Well, he seemed interested in Roman history. That was a plus.

"My name is Jack," he told him but before he could ask the boy for his name again, he was already telling him.

"I am Julius. Named in honour of our greatest citizen. Julius Caesar our finest emperor."

"Yeah, yeah, yeah," Jack said scathingly, "You needn't keep the game going now, Julius or whatever your name is. So you're dressed like Julius Caesar and you're going to a fancy dress party, right? Like I believe all that other rubbish right? I've had a pigging horrible day. I've been told off by the teacher and thumped rotten by two kids in my class. I can't go home in case they start on me again. All I need is you mucking about. Go away and leave me alone. Zak and Josh didn't put you up to this did they?"

He was beginning to feel so sorry for himself that he was afraid he might start crying again and no way was this kid going to see him do that. His left arm was really hurting badly and he was shivering from being soaking wet.

"You can play a game with me if you like." Julius offered, totally un-phased by Jack's outburst.

"But you'd better take off some of your clothes and try to dry them in the wind. Empty out your shoes. They are full of water. You should wear sandals like mine then the water would drain out."

"I thought you were supposed to be going to a fancy dress party," Jack snapped back, his voice sullen and whiney.

"That's what you said. I did not understand you. And you notice that I am not rude about your peculiar clothes. While they are drying will you play knuckle-bones with me?"

He bent down to the ground and picked up a handful of smallish stones, studying each one to make sure it was suitable and comparing its size with the others. Reluctantly, Jack realized the boy was right and with difficulty, taking care not to hurt his painful arm, he stripped off his shoes, shirt and trousers and spread them on a nearby bush to dry in the thin warmth of the spring sunshine. Shivering in the slight breeze, he crouched down and frowning thoughtfully, watched the boy. He couldn't believe he was still talking to an odd boy in a dress. It had certainly been a weird day.

He glanced at his watch.

"Ouch!"

He gasped as he crooked his left arm painfully. Despite a soaking his watch still worked.

"I've got to get back. My Dad will worry."

He'd just have to risk running the gauntlet of Josh and Zak. Julius took no notice and now he was kneeling on the ground sharing the pebbles into two equal piles. There were five pebbles in each pile.

"Here, these are yours," he said offering what looked like the smoothest ones to Jack. "I'll show you."

Placing all five of his on the back of one hand, Julius thrust them up into the air catching just one and leaving the rest where they fell.

"They are called tali and this is the master talus," he informed Jack. "Now watch."

He threw the master into the air, picked up one of the others and caught the master before it touched the ground.

"Using only one hand, you must pick up each one in turn like that," he explained. "Then you pick up two at a time, then four. The first one to retrieve all is the winner."

This time Jack was not impressed.

"It's just five-stones," he said, "My dad taught me that game years ago. I don't see what you've got to call it posh names for."

Jack felt ashamed. He knew he was treating the boy badly but he couldn't help it. No-one else was going to have the chance of getting one up on him. Still, this kid hadn't hurt him. He began to feel a bit guilty.

"What's your real name?" he asked quite politely. "Where do you live?"

"I already told you. Julius. I live with my family in the town over there." He pointed further on to the island.

"We just have one of the insulae here but when we return to Rome we shall have a beautiful domus."

"Huh?" Jack pulled a funny face at yet more strange words.

"You're loony," he said, but something, he didn't know what, made him feel scared. He licked his lips nervously again tasting salt.

"Look, I've got to go. My dad's expecting me."

Backing away he still kept a steely eye on Julius, as if he was afraid that he was going to start hurting him or have some sort of hold over him. He felt really spooked by him now. Better be polite, he thought, just in case.

"Sorry, I can't stop to play."

He started to back off ready to run. Julius stared at the odd way Jack was holding his painful arm.

"You have blood on your face and your arm seems hurt. What has happened? Were you in a fight?"

Jack nodded slowly. Should he tell the boy? He would like to tell someone.

Julius said, "I too have had recent fights with other boys in my town. They wrongly accused me of cheating and now many boys fight me. It is not the Roman way my paterfamilias says, but we are not in Rome. We are in Britannia. Here even our own people behave oddly. I am often sad here. I understand your problems."

Suddenly it all came gushing out. He didn't know why he trusted him but falteringly Jack told Julius about Josh and Zak. And the other kids who sided with them. And his mother and father's divorce. It was a great relief to get the whole thing off his chest. Julius nodded understandingly.

"I have had similar troubles," he admitted. "It's the reason I want my family to return to Rome."

Jack felt relieved to have shared his hidden thoughts. Julius didn't seem quite so odd any more in spite of the strange words. This time, when he asked a question, Jack was polite.

"What's a paterfamilias?"

"He is the head of our household and my father. He too will worry if I do not return immediately."

Julius gathered up his pebbles.

"Perhaps we shall play another day," he said, his voice friendly. Jack shrugged.

"Yeah. OK. Maybe. All I ever wanted was to be left in peace. I just want the bullies to leave me alone."

"I too want the same. Peace. We Romans say 'pax'. If we meet again we must each say to each other, 'pax vobis'. In your language, 'peace to you' ".

One-armed, Jack began to put his clothes back on, pulling a face as the cold, still damp clothes stuck to his body. He turned to go then turning back with the intention of saying goodbye he was surprised to find himself alone.

"Julius," he called, "Where are you?"

There was no reply. Jack called again. Silence. He shrugged, then a thought struck him.

'Maybe it's me that's gone loony. Maybe the bullies have thumped me so hard my brain's gone rotten and I just imagined that boy. What if it never really happened and I've gone mad?'

Trudging back with squelching shoes along the path, he kept turning and straining his eyes in the direction that Julius had said that he lived but there was no-one in sight.

Then a thought struck Jack.

"This is Two Tree Island. A little bit of grassy land sticking out into the sea in Essex. People just don't live here," he cried aloud.

And then he thought, no way, not in a million years, was there a town on it. Julius had said he came from a town but had not named it. If it had been Leigh or Southend, he would have said so but they were in the opposite direction to where

Julius had pointed. Jack felt a shiver run down his back. Of course it was all in his imagination.

He was freezing cold and a lot later than he should have been. Dad was going to get really mad at him. He began to run.

CHAPTER 3

"Where have you been?" Jack's father shouted, opening the door as Jack ran down the path.

"Bad enough I'm late. I thought you'd be home from school ages ago. When I found you weren't in I..."

"Sorry Dad," Jack mumbled, keeping his head down and trying to hide the scratches and bruises that he had got from the going over Zak and Josh had given him. He attempted to squeeze past his dad but Bob Page had wedged his body firmly in the doorway and Jack couldn't get through.

"What have I told you about not going anywhere without letting me know?"

His father was starting to sound angry now.

"I even phoned your mother to make sure you'd gone to school this morning. I'd better let her know you're OK."

His dad sounded cross. As he moved to go indoors his father noticed the marks on Jack's face and the odd way he was holding his arm.

"What's happened? Are you hurt?" Now he was concerned not cross.

"No I'm fine Dad, just fell over that's all and I hung around on the cliffs watching the gulls over on Two Tree Island."

It wasn't exactly lying but not exactly the truth. Jack did not want to tell his father about being bullied or being too frightened to walk home. Dad had got enough worries.

"You're holding your arm oddly," his dad said tugging at his sleeve."Ye-ow!" Jack let out a howl as a searing pain shot through his arm.

"Something's up." He put an arm on the boy's shoulder encouragingly. "You'd better tell me the truth."

Jack thought quickly. Telling the truth without mentioning all the facts was not easy but he tried.

"I fell over on the way home and my elbow hit the pavement." That was enough information he thought, managing not to mention Zak or Josh or bullying. If his father went up to the school and complained it would only make the boys thump him about more and the rest would have a go at him for snitching. It was best to keep quiet.

His father said firmly,

"Get in the car and we'll go up to the hospital. I'm not taking chances. You might have broken it."

Jack was surprised his father didn't complain about his wet clothes but on checking was amazed to find they had already dried. Were bone dry in fact, as were his shoes. At that time though, he didn't give it another thought.

The accident and emergency waiting room at the hospital was packed. It would be a long wait and Jack was hungry. He put his good hand into his trouser pocket in the hope of finding something to eat and pulled out the old coin he'd picked up on Two Tree Island. He looked at it more closely. He could just make out the shape of a head with a sort of crown but it was old and dirty.

"Jack Page." The voice penetrated his thoughts. Jack shoved the coin back into his pocket. A nurse led him and his father behind a heavy plastic screen.

"The doctor's ready for you now."

The doctor prodded and twisted Jack's arm about then said,

"Well Lad, looks like you've broken it. Better get it plastered."

There was still more waiting about before having his arm covered in plaster of Paris. It felt incredibly heavy as he and his father headed back towards the hospital car park.

"Do you fancy stopping for some fish and chips?" his father asked. Jack nodded. He was still hungry.

After supper, Jack went straight to bed, exhausted after the weird day. Jumbled dreams disturbed him and he woke early the next morning.

"I'll ring the school," his dad told him, "And tell them you'll need the day off. Now, give that arm a rest and don't do anything silly while I'm at work!"

When his dad had left, Jack read for a bit then watched TV but he couldn't concentrate. He was bored. He stared out of the window. It was a bright, sunny morning, not the sort of day he wanted to spend indoors.

'I'll just go for a walk,' he thought, 'Dad wouldn't mind that.'

Deep in thought, Jack found himself heading for Two Tree Island. Now he was again sitting on the gnarled wood stump by the water's edge. His tummy rumbled hungrily and he felt in his pocket to see if there were any sweets. Once more he found the old coin. He took it out and tried rubbing it clean.

CHAPTER 4

Thump! Thump! Thump!

"What's that?"

Jack was aware of a rhythmic noise getting louder and louder all the time. He looked up to see if there was a low-flying aircraft coming in to land at Southend airport after crossing the Channel, but there wasn't. Now he was nearly deafened by the thunderous sound that seemed to surround him. He glanced round.

"Wow!"

There, immediately behind him were hundreds and hundreds of men marching and all dressed alike.

The cars had all gone. The hordes passing him through the now empty car park, marched rhythmically, heavily, noisily, their armour clanging.

Jack sat there unnoticed. He could see that each man was dressed in some sort of woollen tunic with his chest covered in a breast plate made out of metal. Some had strips of metal and some had rings. Soldiers! Each wore a helmet, some were shiny and looked to be made of metal too, with pieces that came down low over their eyes and down the sides of their faces. Others were lighter, made of a different material, maybe leather. Each man carried a heavy pack bag and most of them held weapons in their right hands. Weapons that looked like javelins.

"Greetings Jack. Pax vobis. Look at that. They are home and victorious. They have returned from Gaul."

Julius had materialised from nowhere.

"Julius," Jack gasped, "It's you! You are real! Where have all those men come from? There must be thousands of them!"

"Roman soldiers returning victorious from battle. They have conquered Gaul and the Germanic peoples too."

"Wha..at?" Jack doubled up with laughter, rolling off the piece of wood and thumping on to the ground on his bottom.

"Don't be stupid," he began, but he could see that Julius was deadly serious and the more he watched the procession of marching men, the more what Julius said seemed possible. Jack glanced again at the marching men and they looked exactly like the pictures of Roman Centurions in the school history books.

"Wow!" he said, almost believing Julius at last, "Wow!"

"Come on," Julius whispered, "Follow me."

As the last of the long line of soldiers passed by, Julius tagged behind them, half crouching down so he wouldn't be seen. Jack, frightened that Julius would disappear again and leave him on his own, leapt to his feet and followed.

"Poo! It stinks here," he complained sidestepping great lumps of horse droppings. At the end of the column of soldiers were twelve uniformed men riding enormous white horses.

"Ssh!" warned Julius, worried about being discovered, "They are some of the cavalry. They are messengers and spies. Most of them are at the front of the column but these are bringing up the rear. It's tradition."

The smell from the horses was strong but Julius, more used to it than Jack, didn't seem affected by them. Nor by the steam rising in clouds from their sweating bodies and flaring nostrils. The noise of hooves behind them made both the boys leap out of the way to the side of the roadway.

"Oh God! What are they?" Every new sound made Jack jump.

A huge basket-weave cart on four wooden wheels was being pulled along by a pair of yak-like animals. These were braced together by a strong leather yoke and led by a helmeted soldier. As it trundled past, the boys could see it was loaded with sacking bags, bulging with supplies. Sticking up on end, above the side of the cart, was a stack of spears, their blades glinting in the sunlight. Many of the blades were stained red and dripping.

"Wow!" Jack gasped and then, realising what it was, "Ugh, it's blood!"

He felt sick rise in his throat but Julius was pulling him onwards.

"Come on," urged Julius, dragging his friend by his good arm, to join behind the procession again. "It's just blood spilled in war," he explained, then, "Let's follow them back and see if we can creep into the fort without being seen. I have longed for this chance."

Jack panicked. He might enjoy history but not this much.

"I just want to go home!" He whinged, but where was that now? His feet felt like lead as he forced himself to follow Julius and join the end of the route march to be led into the unknown.

"Many of these men have a long journey to make. Even though they are back here in Britannia, they must now travel to the fort on Hadrian's Wall. The fort at Vindolanda. Their route march will be much further than the one they have just taken from the coast at the south. They joined the southern ranks before the army set off for Gaul so as to increase the Roman numbers."

Julius sounded more like a history teacher than a kid. "How do you know all this stuff?" Jack interrupted.

Julius obviously had plenty more information but Jack knew he wouldn't be able to tell Julius what the British army was up to, if things were the other way round.

"How do you know so much about the Roman army, Julius?" The question went unanswered.

All this time they had shuffled along the dusty track behind the Roman troops.

"Arrest! Arrest!"

Now, deafening shouts echoed back from the commanding soldiers at the front, repeated at intervals like massive Chinese whispers so the hundreds of men, bringing up the back half of the column, could be told what to do.

Gradually through the ranks, the men halted until those on horseback in front of the boys stopped too, as did the yaks. Julius nervously held his finger to his mouth.

"Don't speak. Say nothing," he commanded.

The column of men slowly moved forward again, the horses' hooves clip-clopping at a walking pace, their metal shoes ringing loudly against the cobble stones. Jack watched the men disappear under an archway set in a hugely high, enormously wide wall.

"The fort!" Julius announced excitedly. "We're here."

"Wow!" Jack repeated, excited and frightened at the same time.

"This is one of our largest forts," Julius informed him, "It covers twenty hectares and houses about five thousand men."

"It can't do." Jack was puzzled. "Two Tree is just a tiny island. It's not big enough for a few people to live on, never mind a huge great camp like that."

Julius obviously thought Jack was a bit stupid.

"What do mean island? This is no such thing. This is the coast of south-east Britannia. We wouldn't settle on some tiny island. Although Britannia is a tiny island to us, for we are the mighty Roman Empire."

Jack thought it best to keep quiet. He didn't want to upset Julius. After all he wasn't exactly well off for friends but there was a limit and Julius was decidedly odd.

"Quick!" Julius yanked him down by his good arm so that they were crouching next to the basket weave cart as it trundled forward. Jack noticed the muck and slime from the roadway had splashed over his clothes. His dad'd have a go at him for that.

"Keep down below the top so that legionary can't see us." Julius pointed to a soldier on the other side of the cart who was checking in the troops.

"If we can get past him we will be in unseen. The others will be going off to eat. Just don't let that Marius's mule see us."

"Mule! You mean a donkey? " Jack gasped the question. He couldn't deal with any more stinky animals or their smelly droppings.

"No! It's what they call legionaries. They're named after General Marius. He was a consul and that's their nickname. Ssh! Keep down. The gates are closing. Jack! We're in. It's what I've always wanted. When I'm a centurion...."

"Halt!"

A giant of a Roman soldier, towering over them menacingly thrust his spear angrily towards them, barring their way. Both boys cowered in fear, their bodies shaking. The man stared at them, his piercing eyes taking in all the details. He prodded the sharp pointed head of his spear aggressively towards Julius. Then he spoke gruffly, his face brushing frighteningly close.

"And what boy is this who infiltrates our fort?"

CHAPTER 5

"Sir. Please Sir...."

Julius was tugging at the soldier's tunic as Jack cowered in a corner of the musty room.

"Cease boy!!!"

The huge man's Roman uniform swirled and clanged as he moved and his thunderous voice blasted their ear-drums. From his great height he stared angrily down his large Roman nose into Julius' pleading face.

"Sir, Sir, by Jupiter and Neptune, I mean no ill. Pax vobis, Sir. I mean no harm, only peace" Julius pleaded.

"Waaaahhhh!" The huge soldier opened wide his enormous mouth and let out a great guffaw of laughter so loud that Jack's ear drums hurt and he covered his ears with his hands.

Julius was shaking. He had never seen a man so huge before. All Roman men, the ones he knew, were muscular and stocky, like his father, like his grandfather, like Julius Caesar himself. Not tall but thick-set, with hair the colour of his mother's ginger cakes. This giant of a man with his black hair, tangled beard and eyebrows like bushes, put fear in his very insides.

"You speak?" The man boomed. "You assure me of your peaceful intentions. But why should I believe you?"

Again the man hooted with laughter, apparently amused at Julius's words. The soldier's language sounded foreign and very strange to Jack and he didn't understand a word. Yet, strangely, he knew what Julius was saying all the time.

"Please Sir, this is Jack. He is no threat to the fort. He is my friend. He is just one of the Bagglies, the wild men Britons. He has befriended me."

The soldier stared hard at Julius as if he was stupid, stabbing roughly at the boy's body with the blunt end of his weapon. Julius bit his lip in pain, but noticed the soldier was totally ignoring Jack. Pulling harshly at the material at the neck of Julius' tunic, the soldier asked menacingly,

"And who are you boy that steals unbidden into our fort? A thief or just a scallywag?"

"Sir, I wish to be a centurion. I wish to learn."

Julius' voice had risen to a squeak in his fear. He knew he must be brave. He cleared his throat and began again.

"Rough boys have set upon me, Sir and near broken my bones. My friend Jack here has been hurt too, Sir." He again indicated Jack who was cowering on the floor.

"It is the way of the Bagglies too, Sir."

The huge Roman shook his head, appearing not to understand. He made an enormous guttural sound deep down in his throat. Jack felt sick. His stomach heaved but he couldn't stop staring at the soldier's spear. It was so near Julius' flesh he was sure his friend would be killed at any moment. His teeth chattered loudly and even if he'd wanted to he couldn't have uttered a word.

Gathering up all his strength Jack began to run towards the other end of the room where stacks of blood-stained spears stood in scruffy barrels. Pulling with all his might he dislodged one from the edge of the stack and lifted it out of the barrel, dragging it back towards the Roman's feet.

"Take that! And that! And that!" He yelled.

Whack! Whack! Whack! He thrust the spear as hard as he could at the soldier's ankles. The soldier leapt in the air, the skirt of his tunic flaring this way and that.

"Ow! Ow! Ow!" he cried, "What rat attacks my legs, what vermin dares to bite me?"

"Leave him alone, stop hurting my friend!" screamed Jack forgetting to be frightened. Again he attacked the Roman's ankles, thumping him as hard as he could but the soldier peering over his huge stomach, didn't seem to see him.

"Dratted rats!" yelled the man, leaping about all over the place as if he was performing a mad dance.

The soldier, having mistaken the thwack of the spear for some biting animal, looked down to the floor expecting to see a rodent-like creature there and was surprised to find nothing.

Julius, taking advantage of the giant letting go of him, grabbed Jack's good arm and dragging him along behind, made a dash for the door.

"Halt Boy!"

Jack couldn't understand the soldier's words but he knew instinctively from his aggressive tone that they must stand still.

Getting ahead of them, the soldier's body filled the doorway. His bushy, matted beard almost covered his face and the top of his metal armour that he still wore, bore the blood stains of recent battle. The boys could smell a pungent odour as they got near to him, a smell of horse sweat and manure. Jack guessed that he had been one of the army of soldiers, which had thundered past them earlier.

Now the man was again pointing the spear at Julius and as he waggled it, the blade flashed, catching the light from the window. He grabbed Julius by the scruff of his neck and thrust him high above his head at arms length so his head scraped against the rough, cob-webbed ceiling of the building.

"Put me down! Let me go! You're hurting me! Put me down!" screamed Julius in terror as the man sneeringly laughed up at him. He spat out words that Jack again, couldn't understand.

Panting with fear, Jack asked,

"Julius, what's he saying?"

Julius looked scared and was reluctant to tell. Eventually he whispered,

"He says I am like a dog with a broken paw and he should break my other paws and feed me to the lions."

Jack felt himself gag. He daren't be sick. If he puked on the man they'd have no hope. The soldier would really carry out his threat to Julius.

"What is your business here?" the man boomed to Julius in a voice so loud that it again blasted into Jack's ear-drums.

"You should not be in the fort and yet I see from your attire that you are one of us Romans and not a wild-man Briton. Who are you?"

"My name is Julius, Sir. I am the son of...."

"A worthy name. So, your father is here in the fort. In that case all is well."

He let Julius drop to the ground and went on,

"However, you should touch nothing in this room. These weapons are dangerous and for men only. Soon the men will be gone and the fort will be used for training boys. Boys who wear the green uniform and soon will have the honour of wearing the red sash. Boys who will become soldiers. Now I must go to the temple to pray to the God Mithras. Your father has taught you of this?"

Julius nodded dumbly.

Jack, still feeling shaky and nauseous, huddled in close

to the wall trying to keep in the shadows. Although things seemed better, he thought Julius was still scared of the huge soldier and his booming voice.

When the soldier had left, Jack said shakily,

"I don't understand what has happened. I'm scared. Everything's peculiar and I don't..." He couldn't get any further. He looked puzzled and frightened.

"We certainly need to get something explained," Julius commented in an offhand voice, "You're so frightened all the time and you don't know anything, well not the things you ought to know and you're still wearing very odd clothes which cannot help when the soldiers see you."

"I was just thinking the same about you," Jack retorted, "And then all the soldiers and horses came along and you seemed to know exactly what was going on." Suddenly realisation dawned.

"I knew it. I guessed. Yeah! I knew it all the time. You're an actor and you've got an important part in a film haven't you? Well! I know you have to live the part but you're just taking it too far. I'm fed up with all this play-acting. It might all seem OK to you but... Anyway, what I don't get is where are the cameras?" he shrugged his shoulders and looking lost, went on in a whiney voice,

"My arm hurts a lot....and I just want to go home."

By now he looked so miserable that Julius thought he was going to cry.

"We need to talk," he said in quite an adult voice, "But first let's explore."

"Oh no! We'd better get out of here." Jack was horrified at the thought of staying there any longer.

"I don't want any more soldier-actor blokes to find us. They look mean and so do the weapons. You could see blood stuff all dried up on the ends of the spears. I know it's just paint but it's all too real even if they are just actors. No! I just want to get out. I wish I hadn't followed you in here at all."

His voice was quivering.

"Perhaps we could come back and explore another day," he finished lamely.

Now Julius was looking puzzled.

"We haven't gone to such effort to get in just to leave again so soon and anyway I need to ask you, what does OK mean?"

Jack shook his head and shrugged his shoulders again. At least when Julius was being stupid like this, it stopped him feeling frightened and thinking too much about the predicament they were in. Whoever hadn't heard of saying OK? What a dope! Ridiculous.

"Is your father really here?" Jack asked trying to get back to a normal situation.

"No, the soldier just thought he was, so we were in luck."

"And what was that stuff about praying to some god?"

"Mithras was the God of youth and strength and the victory of life over death. Many soldiers worship him as he will help to make them brave in battle. Surely you have learnt that in school."

"Yeah, yeah. We learn about all that stuff at my school all the time. NOT."

Julius was moving silently.

"Keep close to the wall," he told Jack. "Follow me along this corridor."

He was keen to explore but ready at any moment to run in case some angry soldier should discover them. Jack, because he had no other option, followed close on his heels copying his every action. He was in a completely foreign world. Even the disembodied voices of shouting, jeering, merrymaking soldier actors didn't make sense because he couldn't make out what they were saying.

The fort was protected by a strong, high wall and most of the way round, a deep ditch.

"We must hope that the gate we came in by is open for some reason, otherwise it means a long wait," Julius said. "And then we must hide somewhere inside the perimeter of the wall, possibly until long after dark, before we risk escape."

Shinning up the rough surface of the wall and trying somehow to climb down the other side, was out of the question.

Jack was desperate to get home but he had only one useable arm and they would need rope or some strong material at least, for that sort of escape.

"Please Julius get us out of here," he began, not caring now if he sounded like a frightened baby. However, before Julius could reply, a door was flung back sharply so that it crashed resoundingly against the wall. The sound of raised voices and clunking metal, meant soldiers were on the way back.

"Please let's get out of here. I'll promise I'll come again if you want to." Jack knew he didn't mean it.

"I know it's stupid to be frightened on a film set but those soldiers look real even if they are just actors. Come on. Let's go."

In any case, even on a film set they could be in trouble for trespassing. Keeping close in to the walls, they left the building they had been in and darted in the direction of the gate, past two other small buildings.

"That's the sports arena in there. We call it the gymnasium," whispered Julius, "and that's the temple." He pointed to yet another building. "Now you tell me something. What's a film set? Oh!" He didn't wait for an answer. "We're in luck, ssh!"

He dropped suddenly to his knees behind a large, sprouting

bush and Jack copied him. Several men were leaving the temple and heading out of the fort.

Clang! The heavy gates swung open to let them out. The two boys shadowed the men, who were talking excitedly and did not notice them.

Jack again followed Julius's lead. As the gatekeeper clanged the gates shut once more, the boys sank down on to the grass beneath the high wall, on the outside of the fort.

Giggling hysterically, they rolled over and over on the grassy slope that ran downwards from the high fort wall, Jack taking care not to roll on his plastered arm.

Still giggling breathlessly, they came to an abrupt halt by the shallow ditch at the bottom.

"I can't believe we were actually in there," Jack whispered, still scared to speak in a normal voice for fear of being heard. "I didn't know they were making a film. It's clever the way the actors keep in character isn't it? They were so real I s'pose I was a bit scared."

Now they were out, Jack started to be a bit cocky about everything he'd seen.

Julius said,

"It has been exciting but we saw very little. To know what my future as a centurion holds, I need to return and see much more."

"Look," Jack said in rather an exasperated tone, "You really don't have to keep this up."

"What do you mean?"

"All this pretending to be Roman stuff. Anyway, how do you think they did all that display? Lasers and stage make-up I suppose. You'd never guess there was a film studio on Two Tree Island. I've not seen it advertised anywhere. When I get home, I'll ask Dad if he knows anything about...."

"Jack you are talking in riddles now. I am Roman. There's no pretending in that." Julius looked quite hurt that his new friend would even think so.

"OK Mate. Well let's pretend we're getting back to the twenty-first century now eh?" Jack's tone was sarcastic, "Or my Dad will have my guts for garters if I'm late again. He worries about me."

There was an explosive silence. Julius's mouth opened to say something, then closed again. He frowned. Trying unsuccessfully to speak again he stared at Jack with a body-piercing glare.

"Wha...what day is it today Jack?" he stammered, almost as if he was afraid of his companion. "What is the date?" There was panic in his voice.

Jack sensed that something had changed in Julius's behaviour towards him.

"What's up? What have I done? Oh don't you go turning against me now!" he muttered.

Maybe he had upset the other kids at school and that was why they picked on him all the time. He desperately did not want to spoil things. He jumped up and held a hand out to Julius, intending to help him to his feet.

"Come on," he said. It was a friendly gesture. Julius, ignoring Jack's offer, got up by himself and made a deliberate move to back away from him. He seemed to be suddenly wary of Jack, almost as if he was frightened of being with him.

"The date is um," Jack thought for a minute, "The fifteenth of March."

"But the year, tell me the year." Julius sounded odd as he spoke.

"Don't be daft," Jack giggled, then seeing the look on his friend's face, said seriously, "Two thousand and eleven," and then for some peculiar reason, added, "A.D."

Now it was obvious that Julius did not believe him and again was frightened to be standing near him. Jack saw the other boy back away further. Suddenly Julius gasped,

"The fifteenth, the Ides, that means the full moon. 'Tis a time of evil portent. I should have known."

Giving Jack one more fearful stare, he darted away from him, running as fast as he could.

Not understanding how he had scared him, Jack began to run after him.

"Julius, Julius, come back. Pax vobis, pax vobis!" he cried desperately but as his voice was carried away on the wind, Jack realised that he was once again alone, skirting the car park on Two Tree Island. The fort and the soldiers were nowhere to be seen.

Over on Leigh Hill, the open top bus was chugging its way along on its first journey of the coming summer season. A couple of passengers, kids on their way home from school, were braving the windy March day on the upper deck. Cars, not carts were zooming along the cliff-top. Everything seemed normal. Jack slowly made his way home.

CHAPTER 6

As he turned into his road, Jack could see his father's van on the drive. He broke into a run.

"Dad!" he yelled as he opened the front door. "Dad!"

"Tea's on," his father called. "What have you been doing all day? It's school for you tomorrow or they'll...."

"Dad, they're filming on Two Tree Island. There's a new studio and I've been..."

"Rubbish!" His father interrupted. "I've been down there to the council tip for the last hour getting rid of all those old wood-wormed planks from the job I'm on. I didn't see anything and...."

"You were down there today?"

"I've just told you. Some kids were flying model planes and a group of bird-watchers were dug in but there wasn't any film studio."

"Are you sure?"

"Did you know they call them twitchers?"

"What film-makers?"

"Don't be stupid. Bird-watchers. Anyway, listen, I've got something I want to tell you."

Jack frowned. His dad sounded a bit odd. Sort of nervous and not like his usual self at all.

"What is it, Dad?"

His father cleared his throat as if he was about to make a

speech.

"I've been late home a few times recently," he began but Jack interrupted,

"That's OK. It's better for us when you've got a lot of work on. I don't mind. I can look after myself 'til you get back."

"That's just it, Son. Sometimes it is because I'm working late but sometimes it's because I've stopped to have a cup of tea with a friend."

Jack was puzzled. What was all the fuss about? His dad went on,

"Jack, it's a lady friend. Stacey her name is. She's very nice. We've become close."

"You mean you've got a girl-friend Dad?" Jack was surprised. He hadn't guessed it. It seemed a bit odd but Mum had a new husband, why shouldn't Dad have a girl-friend?

Jack put his good hand into his pocket. The old coin that he had picked up on Two Tree Island was still there. Somehow it was reassuring. He looked at his father,

"It's OK. Dad," he said.

He ate his meal in silence, his mind racing. Everything was changing. First Mum, now Dad and then there was Two Tree Island and Julius. Was that all just in his imagination? No, it couldn't be.

"I've got something for you." His dad interrupted his thoughts. "Here you are."

Jack was amazed. His father was handing him a new mobile phone.

"Cor Dad! Thanks!"

"Well I'm not sure I'm doing the right thing but you've had me on edge recently. I never know where you are or if the old phone'll work. It's a modern one. Takes pictures and that. It's got some new-fangled computer thing too. Before you go wandering off now you've got to let me know. OK. Son? Keep me in touch. That's what it's for. So if I'm late home or you're late home, we keep in touch. Yes?"

"Dad it's brilliant!"

"And you should phone your mother sometimes. I've had an ear-bashing from her today. She says you don't talk to her during the week. No excuses now."

Later, in his bedroom, Jack studied the booklet that came with the phone. He checked the details. How to work the camera. How to use the charger unit. Most importantly, he made a note of his number. He was well pleased. They wouldn't make fun of this one. Might try to pinch it though.

He lay on his bed, deep in thought. Two Tree Island. Had he really heard, seen, smelled and experienced all those things? Julius seemed real enough. Unless he, Jack, was going mad. Maybe Josh and the others had hurt him so badly they'd sent his brain mad, or, or.......or maybe somehow he had..... he couldn't find the proper thoughts to put it into words. Or maybe, just maybe he had really travelled back in time to Roman days. He giggled. Nah! That was stupid.

He took the coin out of his pocket and looked at it. Maybe it was a proper Roman coin but it was too dirty and the markings too flattened to tell. He would have to clean it up. Maybe the coin was the key and could give him some answers.

"Flipping hell!" he said aloud. "I reckon it's all real! I reckon I was really there." He giggled again, nervously this time.

He turned his thoughts to the next day.

"Oh God! I've got to go back to school!"

Still, Jack felt braver about it. After all they couldn't risk thumping him while his arm was in plaster could they?

Next morning, deep in thought about how to get back and

find Julius, Jack ambled down the school path towards the building. There was a bit of a commotion going on near the bike sheds.

"Get off you cow!" One of the girls, a rather fat year eight pupil was fighting off three or four others who appeared to be knocking her about. Another was taking pictures of the action with her mobile phone. No-one was helping her.

"Don't look so worried Jack." It was Zenith. "If anyone can stand up for herself it's Chelsea. Although I didn't think things'd get that bad. Happy slapping comes to the comp!"

Zenith moved on towards the door, leaving Jack alone. As he reached the bike sheds someone grabbed his good arm and jerked him sharply forwards, wrong-footing him and bringing him crashing to the ground on his face. Mud and grit filled his mouth mixing with blood from a cut to the side of his head. He spat, trying to clear his mouth and gasped for air. He winced as he jarred the plaster-covered elbow.

"Here's our little teacher's pet. Not so flaming clever when you're on your own Einstein, without Miss then are yer?"

It was Zak Dreyfus taunting him but it was Josh Smith who had attacked him. It was obvious that Zak was doing it to impress Josh. That's what most of the bullies did stuff for. To impress Josh. Josh was Mr. Big.

"What did you tell that teacher?"

"Yesterday. Did you snitch?"

"You know what happens to kids that snitch doncha?"

"Yeh! Heads down the bog time, yeah? Snitch means head down bog. Remember. We're watching you!"

Pushing him away roughly, they ran off laughing. Jack scrambled to his feet and brushed himself down as best he could with one arm, relieved it wasn't Monday. In any case he'd decided to go to his Mum's with less stuff in future.

The day dragged. He couldn't concentrate on lessons. Apart from the Julius issue, there was making sure he was never anywhere alone where Zak or Josh could get at him. He avoided going to the toilet all day to the point where he was busting. He wasn't going to risk being shoved head first down there.

As soon as school was out, Jack belted for the door determined to outrun the bullies. Within minutes he was safely on the pathway over Leigh train station and running across the car park on the Island. He located the old wood stump, sat on it to get his breath back and looked around.

Everything was still twenty-first century.

"Julius!" he called and louder, "Julius!"

Nothing.

"Julius," he was shouting now, at the top of his voice, "Pax vobis. I believe you. I believe you're Roman. Come on. Where are you? I'll be a Baggly. I'll do anything you want. Come on!"

Jack noticed two little kids about five or six years old, staring at him. Their parents got out of their car and pulled them away, whispering something.

"I don't care if you think I'm mad. I know what I know," he yelled.

All that was important was finding Julius again. The two children stared back at him over their shoulders. Jack stuck his tongue out at them.

Dejectedly, Jack began to trudge back towards the end of the car park. He'd had his chance. A chance in a zillion and he'd lost it. He'd never be able to link on to that point in time again. He'd never see Julius again. His only friend and he'd lost him for ever.

Jack's face was still sore from the going over that morning.

His clothes were dirty and his trousers, new school trousers, had a hole in the right knee. His father would be livid. Luckily he was working late that evening and Jack had time to go home and sort things out. He'd wear his old school trousers tomorrow and try and get the new ones mended without telling his Dad.

"I'll phone Mum up. She'll sew them or something," he muttered to himself as he ambled along. His cut face started bleeding a bit so he felt in his pocket for a handkerchief. There wasn't one. In fact, there wasn't anything at all except his new mobile phone, which he'd only just put there. The trousers were new. Nothing in the pockets. NOTHING IN THE POCKETS! Realisation dawning, he began to sprint, his feet hardly touching the ground.

The coin. The Roman coin. That's what would do it. It would get him in. But it was in the pocket of his old trousers.

With no thoughts of Zak or Josh, he belted home at a sprinter's pace though to Jack it felt as if it took forever. He fumbled his key in the lock and pelted upstairs to his bedroom. His old trousers weren't on the floor where he'd dumped them. He flung open the wardrobe and shoved hangers back and forth.

They weren't there either. Maybe Dad had put them out for a wash.

In the bathroom, the wash-bin was empty. Panic bubbling up, Jack ran down the stairs two at a time and raced into the kitchen. The washing machine was loaded and ready to run. His father must have got it sorted before going off to work. Jack clicked the door open praying that the clothes hadn't already been put through the wash cycle.

What if they were wet? If the coin had been soaked in twenty-first century detergent, would it still hold the power that Jack was sure would get him back to Roman Britain?

Gingerly he touched the first piece of clothing. Dry! He yanked everything out on to the floor. A whole week's dirty washing. The last thing to fall out was his dirty school trousers. Falteringly he felt in the pockets. Empty!

Dejectedly, one arm hanging by his side, Jack shovelled the lot back into the machine. Now what? Where was the coin? Of course, Dad made sure all the pockets were empty so what would he have done with the coin?

Jack eyed the waste bin and wrinkled his nose. Potato peelings, old banana skins, scraped off baked beans, the remains of a Chinese take-away, a smelly old thrown out floor cloth.

Could the coin be in there? Or would Dad just have chucked it out into the dustbin? Jack eyed the washing machine again. An idea occurred to him. Once again, with his one good arm, he dragged the contents out on to the floor and felt around inside. It was there! He touched it! His hand felt it, round and hard! The coin had dropped out of his pocket and into the bottom of the machine.

"YEAH! YEAH! YEAH!" He whooped with glee. "Got it!"

With the speed of lightning, he tidied up the mess so his Dad wouldn't suspect anything and set off back to the path by Leigh train station and, he hoped, the road to Roman times.

CHAPTER 7

Jack dipped the coin in the sea water that was lapping at his feet. He rubbed it against his trouser leg to remove as much dirt as possible and thought about Julius. Then it happened.

"Hail Jack. Pax vobis. I am so happy to see you for I know you are a true friend."

Julius's voice was so weak and wobbly and he looked so different that Jack hardly recognized him. His shoulders drooped as he walked towards him and Jack could see that Julius was in pain. His head was bandaged and he too wore a rough splint on his left arm. Like Jack, his face was scratched and bloodied.

"Pax vobis." The strange words gave Jack a feeling of power. "What happened? Surely you didn't go back into the fort alone?"

"No! It was the same as with you. What did you call them? Bullies. I was set upon by three bullies, boys who have hurt me before."

Now Julius dropped to the ground and with a stick began scooping up animal droppings and smearing them on to deep cuts on his legs.

"Ugh! That's sick!" Jack exclaimed. "What on earth are you doing? You'll get awful infections if you do that!"

Jack felt like puking as he watched but Julius continued. Weakly he explained.

"It is already infected and it is our way Jack. We cover the wound with animal droppings to encourage insects which will be attracted and eat the rotten flesh so leaving my legs clean. It is what the soldiers do."

Jack grimaced but didn't comment. Instead he said,

"So how did it happen?"

"There is much to tell you. I hoped we would meet again and I have brought papers to prove to you I am Roman."

"No need," Jack said, "I really believe you already. Do you believe I am from the twenty-first century?"

Julius nodded though he didn't look very sure.

They made themselves comfortable on the grassy bank and Julius began,

"My paterfamilias is a medical man. He follows the teachings of the great Greek doctor, Hippocrates. He understands the sciences. He performs many operations. Sometimes I creep into his room and touch the bronze operation tools, sharp knives and tweezers."

Jack nodded but couldn't see what that had to do with a bunch of bullies giving Julius a thrashing.

"Already I have been falsely accused of cheating. I told you this," Julius continued. "It is because the boys are jealous of my background. They say we are a family of wealthy, uncaring Patricians. It is not true. We are not unduly wealthy and my paterfamilias is most caring."

"Yeah, but what's that got to do with...."

Julius nodded but Jack still couldn't see the point Julius was making.

"Have patience my friend. You remember the soldier in the fort told us the fort will now be used to train boy soldiers. My paterfamilias has been appointed doctor to the fort. The boys assume it will give me undue advantage to train as a soldier and succeed without even trying. Of course it will not but still they thrash me."

"So both of us have been bullied for something we haven't done."

"Indeed," Julius agreed, "For no crime at all."

"Perhaps that's why we were sort of..... destined to meet." Jack thought deeply and was quiet for a while. Something was getting worked out inside his brain but for the time being, he decided not to mention it.

Julius went on,

"The fort is to be called Bohaz training school. Boys from our encampments at Capta and Fiery and Facta will come here to train as soldiers."

"I've never heard of such places. Not round here."

Julius fumbled in his tunic and brought out some papers.

"Look. I will show you. These are my proof of who we are."

He un-crumpled the coarse papers and laid them out on the ground. Jack could see they were maps of some sort. There was something familiar about them.

"What's that place?" he asked pointing to a small area of land.

"Capta."

"No it's not. It's Canvey Island. It's just there, in that direction." He pointed. "You can see it from Leigh cliffs."

"And that is Facta and that Fiery."

Julius was pleased to get Jack so interested.

"We call them Wallasea Island and Foulness Island. These are places I know. They are twenty-first century places." Jack was very excited now.

"And also Roman encampments." The boys were thrilled to have found true common ground. Now Jack decided to tell

Julius his idea.

"I have seen what it's like in your world Julius. I have found a way in. What if we could find a way into my world for you?"

"But," Julius's eyes nearly popped out of his head, "But there is not truly a twenty-first century is there?"

Jack stared at him.

"What? D'you think I tell lies? I believed you. Why can't you believe me?"

He had really thought they trusted each other but he was wrong. Jack stomped off across the grass making sure to tread huge footprints on Julius's maps and kick them so the wind took them away. He was livid, angry with himself for trusting Julius.

"I am sorry. I apologise, I believe in you," Julius cried after him but Jack refused to turn round. He had been hurt once too often. He'd never trust anyone again.

Resting against a tree quite a way off from Julius, Jack didn't know what to do next. Thinking about it, he had never actually found his way back home before. It had always been Julius disappearing then the twenty-first century was suddenly there.

"So I can't go back home 'til he decides to call it quits. Bloody hell!"

He knew he shouldn't swear. Dad'd kill him if he found out. But it helped. While he was dithering, not knowing what to do, Jack heard a sound. At home it wouldn't have startled him. At home, it would have been a normal sound. But here? Here it was blooming weird. It was the bleep of his mobile telling him he'd just got a text.

Slowly, because it WAS so weird, Jack took the phone out of his pocket and flipped the lid open.

'RU OK? Where R U? Ring me Mum.'

Jack giggled. Only his mum could text him in Roman Britain.

"Ben must've taught her how to text," he muttered to himself. He giggled again and dialled her number but nothing happened. That scared him because that meant he couldn't get help. He tried texting, wondering whether to say *'Am in Roman Britain wish you were here'* but he just tapped in *'Ring U soon'* and the text went off OK. That meant he could have contact with his own time if he needed it. Weird. Wouldn't the history teacher just love to know about that?

"What are you doing?" It was Julius.

"Wouldn't you like to know?"

Julius stared at the mobile nervously and bravely held his hand out. Jack flipped it to camera mode and handed it to him.

"Go on then. Hold it up and click it. It takes pictures."

Julius did as he was instructed but didn't understand the point. Jack realised he'd need a second mobile to show how the picture was sent between phones. He'd have to think of something else. He pressed 121 and held the phone to Julius's ear.

"You have no messages," the mobile said. It was a woman's voice. Julius frowned and turned the phone over to look underneath. He held it to his ear but no more words came. He shook it hard.

"Oi stop that! You'll break it," yelled Jack grabbing it back from him.

"How did you do that?" Julius was totally mesmerised. "It is magic!"

"No Mate. That's twenty-first century technology not magic." Jack put on a superior voice.

"Now do you believe me?"

Julius nodded enthusiastically.

"Do more tricks please," he begged.

Jack scrolled through until he got the ring tone options. It was the latest model and some of the sounds were weirdly outrageous. Julius laughed aloud and did a head-over-heels across the grass despite the splint on his arm.

"Ouch! That hurt but no matter. Your magic is more important. Yes please. I agree to your idea. I would like to visit your century."

"Oh so you've decided I'm telling the truth now have you?" Jack was still being superior. Then more seriously,

"But how do we get you in?"

"I must see a place where machines can talk. We must find a way."

"We have all sorts of machines that talk," Jack promised, "If I can just find a way to get you in."

CHAPTER 8

They walked on, talking all the time and trying to work out ways of getting Julius into the twenty-first century.

Jack said suddenly,

"We are real friends aren't we Julius?"

Julius nodded.

"True friends," he replied.

"Then I've had an ace idea." By now, Jack was yelling excitedly.

"D'you reckon we could help each other fight the bullies? You're the only person I can trust with all this."

Julius thought deeply then nodded. He spoke in a serious voice.

"We cannot seek help as no-one would believe either of us. What we must do, we must do alone, just the two of us," he said, "but first we must find a trusty way to travel from Roman times to the twenty-first century and back."

"We could try using the same coin I came here with," Jack said.

"Possibly I could wear an item of your clothing," Julius suggested.

"Or we could try sitting on the wood stump. That may work."

"What if you take a good run up first and I follow you and sort of leap into time...."

They chattered on, not realising how far they had gone. Suddenly Jack said,

"Where are we? I don't recognise anything. Are we still on Two Tree?"

"We are far now, from the fort," Julius said.

At that moment both boys heard a thunderous noise.

"What's that? What's happening?" Jack felt panic in his stomach and bile rise in his throat. Instinct told him they were in danger.

"Run Jack! Run fast! Follow me!" Yelled Julius, safe in the knowledge no-one could hear him above the din. He pulled Jack down behind some bushes. Breathlessly both boys peered over the top aghast at what was happening.

Dozens of angry, uniformed soldiers rushed forward, weapons held high, to be confronted by great gangs of what looked to Jack to be cavemen. Shaggy-bearded, rough-skinned men wearing animal skins for clothes, met the Romans head-on in a fight. Julius whispered,

"It's a pitched battle. The soldiers have left the fort to defend the area face to face with the enemy. See over there." He pointed to a group of Romans carrying a giant wooden catapult, which they set down on level ground.

"That's a ballista," Julius said. Jack watched as a soldier loaded it with huge iron bolts and began 'firing' at the local men, who hit back with arrows and stones.

"What if they see us? We'll be killed," he said, petrified.

"Watch, over there." Julius was too excited to be scared as he pointed out another group of soldiers. "That's the tortoise technique."

Now another group of soldiers moved in formation, holding their shields close together above their heads to form a 'roof' of protection. As they moved they looked just like a giant tortoise ambling along. The boys could hear arrows and stones smashing down on the shields and bouncing off. Eventually the local tribesmen were overcome and the survivors scattered. The Romans marched back in the direction of the fort.

"That was scary," Jack said, "Thank goodness they've gone. But where are we?"

"We are near the avenue of the insulae, near my paterfamilias's house. I will show you but you must understand it is not as grand as our domus in Rome."

Jack was getting used to Julius's weird words and understood that he wanted to show him his home but it made him very agitated.

"No Julius, NO!"

"What frightens you now?"

"What if your parents see me?"

Julius smiled.

"They will offer you food and rest. It is our custom." But Jack was not convinced.

"Oh yeah! Look at me. They're hardly going to think I'm one of your Roman mates are they? My clothes, my hair. I won't know what to do. I'll say something wrong, something twenty-first century. They'll probably think I'm dangerous and get me slung in jail or they'll....."

"Stop! Stop!" Julius doubled up with laughter and plonked on the ground. He hadn't seen Jack in this much of a state before.

"Jack you have become a frightened animal that I might see in the zoological gardens I have visited! This is my home. You will be welcome. You must be brave!"

Now Julius was making fun of Jack and they both knew it but it changed Jack's mood. He relaxed. Both boys walked on happily. "Come," Julius turned to beckon Jack on. "Although we are in Britannia, the town is built just as at home. Follow me through this archway and we will enter the Forum."

The two boys walked beneath an amazing, carved archway into a square. Large buildings lined all four sides and there were many different shops and market stalls. It was ablaze with colour and noise, fruit and clothes, shoes and loaves of bread, flowers and brightly coloured ribbons. The stalls and counters overflowed with it all.

"Wow! Look at that!"

Jack twisted and turned this way and that trying to take it all in.

"It looks like Southend market on a Thursday," he said in surprise. "Except for the grand buildings, it looks just like home."

"Except for the people's clothes too."

The crowds of people, mostly men, were wearing flowing white robes. In the middle of the square an important man stood on a raised platform making a speech to a group of onlookers who were surrounding him. There was a drinking fountain just like in the playground at school and kids were slurping and spraying the water. There was even a public lavatory and a sign pointing to another building that Julius explained was the public baths.

"What's that?" Jack asked, pointing to a religious looking painting on one wall.

"That is a shrine. Every forum must have a shrine and every town must have a forum." Julius looked sad. "But In Rome it is far better."

"Everything's wicked!" Jack said. Julius was horrified.

"No! No! It is good." Jack laughed.

"In my time 'wicked' means great. Good. Fantastic. It's fantastic!" he said and he meant it. Jack followed Julius along the street milling with people, worried that they would pick on him or call him names for the clothes he was wearing. Oddly, they didn't seem to notice.

They had been so engrossed in looking at the sights and the to-ing and fro-ing of the crowds of people they had not noticed three boys creeping up on them.

"YAH! YAH! YAH!"

With a wild battle cry the three boys leapt towards them, punching Julius to the ground, hitting him with the sharpened ends of sticks which cracked around his head and made his ears sting.

Jack crouched in a heap on the ground, waiting for the onslaught, the thumping, but it never came. The three bullies viciously laid into Julius, flooring him. They towered over him frighteningly, in a three on one battle that Julius hadn't a hope of winning.

Time and again they nearly trod on Jack but some miracle stopped them. Staring up from his position on the ground, all Jack could see and hear was the vivid green of the tunics that all three boys wore and the strange words they were shouting at Julius. He kept thinking 'oh no! Not again. Not here in Roman times too!'

Still they didn't touch him but he could see Julius was crumpling, unable to fight them off. Bravely, Jack scrabbled his way along the pavement and began pulling at one boy's legs, trying to get him off Julius. He yanked at his ankles, pulling his feet off the ground so the attacker over-balanced and crashed down with an excruciating yell. Even then, they left Jack unharmed. Feeling braver in victory, Jack thrust one leg over the boy's body to hold him down as he attacked a second bully's ankles.

"Run, Augustus, run!" cried one of the three, "There is

something gravely amiss here!"

After a few minutes that felt like a century, the three fled, darting in and out of the thronging crowds unnoticed by others amid so much noise and activity.

"Ow! Ow! Ow! why does everybody keep thumping me. Oh my arm!" Jack had got knocked about, caught in the cross-fire.

"Mine also."

"Are you alright?"

"Are you hurt much?" Jack and Julius asked one another breathlessly, concerned for each other's welfare.

"Who were they and what were they saying?"

"Those are the boys who have attacked me before. Brutus, Augustus and Flavius. They wear the tunic of Bohaz collegiate. They will be centurions one day. They will achieve my dream. But they are not worthy. They are bullies. It is I who wish to become the soldier and by honest means."

"Why did they only attack you? Why didn't they have a go at me too?" asked Jack, "They could see we were together. Unless of course...."

Jack did not finish his sentence. Realisation dawning for both boys, they both leapt in the air in excitement and yelled in unison,

"They didn't see me!"

"You are invisible!"

They both looked up and their eyes met and again both had the same thought.

"The soldier in the fort. He didn't see me either!"

Julius spoke now in a calmer voice, a serious adult sort of a voice.

"That means when you are here in my time, no-one can see you."

"But you can see me can't you Julius?"

"Of course I can see you but I think maybe it is only I that can do so."

CHAPTER 9

Then both boys were quiet for a while as they digested the information.

"Come on," said Julius at last, "We are almost there."

He darted behind a cloth trader's shop beckoning Jack on. They now stood before a previously hidden building.

"This is our home," Julius announced, "Please follow me."

Nervously, Jack followed making a way through the crowds milling in the street outside, still convinced that at any moment someone would actually be able to see him and grab at him. He still stung a bit from getting in the way of the boys' attack on Julius. He didn't think he could stand any more pain.

"Come," Julius encouraged, "See my home and my paterfamilias and my mother."

"What if they can see me?"

Despite this worry, Jack followed and was amazed. The building felt so modern, almost like being in a hotel in his own time. The floor was covered in incredibly intricate tile patterns of vibrant colours and they seemed to be in some sort of great hall, in the centre of which was a sunken pool.

"Wow! Look at that. Your own swimming pool!"

Julius giggled.

"No my friend. That is not truly for swimming. That is the impluvium. You see above, up there, is an opening in the roof.

The light comes through there but so does the rain. Especially in Britannia. It is often rainy here."

"But it's lovely and warm in here."

"There is heat from the hypocaust. Hot air flows under the floor of course."

"Under floor heating. My dad has been wanting that for ages but it's too expensive. That's so odd," Jack could see the funny side, "That the Romans have got it but Dad and me're still waiting. My dad wouldn't half laugh at that."

Julius led him through one of the many doors off the hallway. It was much darker in there but as Jack's eyes became accustomed to the gloom, he could make out several couches set around the room and a long low table that was like a coffee table, in the centre. Lying on one of the couches was a pretty woman that looked a bit like his mum and on another, a man in a toga.

"This is my paterfamilias, Augustus Valens. Valens is our family name," Julius whispered to Jack, then aloud, "It is good to see you Father."

Although Julius spoke in his own language to his parents, Jack always understood him. Julius's father inclined his head towards his son, gave him a quizzical glance and spoke in a deep voice. Jack did not understand the words this time but he could tell from the tone of voice what Julius's father was saying.

"Who were you talking to my son? Are you playing some trick on me? There is no-one there. Why do you mention my name?"

Jack kept his eyes to the ground so as not to meet the man's glance, just in case he became visible to him. Julius was polite to his father in all he said to him. He told him that a strange boy called Jack, whom he'd met near the fort, was safe as a friend despite probably being a Baggly. Jack was getting used to understanding only one side of the conversation and guessing the other.

"This is my mother, Valentinia," Julius whispered, keeping his face turned from his parents. He used the word 'Mater' not mother.

The woman smiled assuming her son was greeting her in an old fashioned way for she had heard her name, despite Julius's whispering. She pulled her son down towards her and kissed his cheek. Her actions made Jack miss his own mother very much but he did not need Julius' introduction. He understood who she was and liked her immediately. He sensed she would have accepted any friend of her son's. She would have liked him.

Julius's father clapped his hands and servants brought huge platters of food and set them on the long table.

Jack, feeling a sudden urge of hunger-pangs, was overwhelmed by the grand food. His mouth was watering.

"Julius, I'm starving. Can I have something to eat too?"

"Ssh! I have an idea," whispered Julius, then loudly to his father, "Pater, may I eat my food outside in the open air?"

His father nodded and instructed the servant,

"My son will eat under the trees in the quadrangle. See that trays of food are brought to him."

"A picnic?" Jack giggled. "Good thinking Julius."

They sat out on seats beneath the trees in a stony, rectangular area behind the building. Servants brought out a feast of food. To Jack's relief, much too much for only one boy.

There was fish and roast meats cooked in honey, fried chicken, many different fruits and vegetables displayed on enormous platters with huge bunches of succulent grapes decorating each dish. Much of the food was covered in rich sauces and Jack was sure he could taste mint and vinegar. The smells were mouth-watering. The thought of the take-aways and burgers he and his dad had lived on since his mum left, made him hungrier than ever for this special food. He ate and ate and ate until he thought he would burst.

After they had eaten, the servants returned to take the dishes away and Jack whispered to Julius that he had to go. He had suddenly remembered that he hadn't told his Dad where he was and he felt in his pocket, to make sure the mobile phone was still there. It was.

The boys entered the house again and went to the couch where Julius's father lay.

"What would he say if he could see me?" Jack questioned. Julius suppressed a giggle. If only his father knew!

Nervously Jack stood next to Augustus Valens and he looked into the man's face. Their eyes seemed to meet properly but of course in reality they did not. The only seeing eyes were Jack's. It was the weirdest moment of Jack's life.

"Farewell," Julius called to his parents then ran to his mother and kissed her. The two boys left the house and began the walk back in the direction of the fort. Julius wanted to run but Jack couldn't manage it. His stomach was too full.

After a while Jack realised he was in an area of Two Tree Island that he recognised.

"I must text Dad," he said, "Or he'll be mad at me when I get back." He looked at Julius

"It's been great today. I wish you lived in my time. You're the best friend I've ever had."

Julius nodded.

"It is the same for me. If we lived in the same time we could help each other with the bullies."

Jack felt that something momentous was about to happen.

Some sixth sense made him panic.

"I'm scared we won't meet again," he said. "What if I can't find the time zone?"

Julius said, "Ensure you have the coin. It bears the head of Julius Caesar. You must keep it safe always. It will let you in."

Jack felt the coin in his pocket and nodded.

"I will work out how to get you into the twenty-first century. There's so much I want to show you. I must find a way."

He took out his mobile and tapped in a text to his Dad. Julius watched, mesmerised. Jack looked at him.

"Would you like to press the send button?" he offered. Julius nodded. He loved the idea of doing magic. He pressed the button.

Both boys gasped simultaneously.

The fort had gone. The fort wall had gone. The soldier guarding the gate had gone. Roman life had gone. A car revved up and accelerated across the car park. An aeroplane banked and began to descend towards the airport. The distant chimes of an ice-cream van jingled out a nursery rhyme tune.

Jack and Julius stood, side by side in the twenty-first century.

CHAPTER 10

"Ohhhhhhhhhh!!"

Julius screamed a prolonged, horrific, terrified scream. He covered his ears with his hands and screwed up his eyes as if he was in terrible pain. He threw himself to the ground and scrabbled his way along until he was wedged against a wall. He folded himself into the tightest ball he could and his face went white.

"What's the matter? Whatever's the matter? Julius, you've gone white. What is it?"

Jack knew it wasn't their sudden arrival in the twenty-first century. That was something they both wanted. It must be something worse, much worse than just time travel.

"That!....that!...." Julius pointed to the tail end of a train in the distance, screeching to a halt into Leigh train station and then up to the sky, at an aeroplane coming down to land at Southend airport.

"Those screaming monsters...what...what... are... they?"

The fear on his friend's face prevented Jack from smiling. Instead he put his good arm on Julius's shoulder and in a quiet, calm voice told him,

"That is a train. People travel in it on the ground, on rails. It takes you fast from place to place. It's not a monster, it's not alive. It is a machine. And that," now he pointed skywards, "that's an aeroplane. Another travel machine. We fly like the birds. You could fly to Rome in one of those."

Julius wasn't convinced but he unfolded his body and risked gradually standing up. Eyes popping out of his head, he slowly looked around, taking in all the new sights and sounds, leaping at Jack for protection as a car zoomed past across the car park.

"It is very noisy here," he said, "That machine rumbles like the Gods in a storm. I am afraid."

"That's a car," Jack informed him, "We travel in those too. Most people have cars. You can have a ride in my Dad's van later."

Julius was shaking too much to reply. Every few seconds he jerked this way and that, looking at some new machine, new noise, strange activity that were everyday things to Jack but to him were the magic even the soothsayers had not managed to predict.

"YOWWWWW!!!!" Now Julius screamed again and began to shake.

"The m..m..magic, the magic!" he stuttered, " It touches me. I am doomed. I shall never see my Mater again. Oh!"

He held his open hand towards Jack, offering him the contents. Jack's mobile phone vibrated and flashed in his palm. Julius moaned softly.

"Oh you dope. It's fine. It's just a text on my phone. Probably my dad wondering where I've got to."

Jack dismissed his friend's fear. If he was totally truthful, he couldn't help thinking how good it felt that it was Julius who felt so scared and not himself. It made a change. Then he thought 'that's mean, he's my friend,' so he said,

"Look Julius, a message from Dad. He says I've got to get my skates on."

Julius frowned not understanding a word, spoken or on the

screen, as Jack showed him the mobile. "It means hurry up," he explained.

With Jack leading the way, the two boys ran helter-skelter across the footbridge and up the cliffs towards Jack's house. Jack un-locked the front door and still breathless from the run, the boys went inside.

"Jack, is that you? I'm in the kitchen," Jack's father called. Jack answered him and headed in that direction. Julius followed behind slowly, gawping at all the strange things that he saw in this strange building of the future. There were huge areas of glass everywhere in the walls that let in the sunshine and the whole place was so bright it made him gasp. Even so, he watched in awe as Jack's hand located a small white lever on the wall, which he pushed downwards. Instantly a bright light shone down from a round shaped object hanging from the ceiling.

"I've put the hall light on," Jack explained, "It's a bit gloomy along here. Dad says the people who had the house before us built the kitchen as an extension and that meant having a long corridor."

Julius shrugged his shoulders. He didn't understand a word.

"Dad we're here. Sorry we're late. I want you to meet my friend...."

But he didn't get any further.

"Yes, you are late. We've got to get to the hospital for your appointment. Your plaster's due off today."

Jack had forgotten.

"That's what I bought your phone for. You're supposed to keep in touch."

His father seemed very agitated and the really odd thing was that he totally ignored Julius. It wasn't like Dad to be rude. Jack tried again.

"Dad, this is ...."

"I think it is the same for me here," Julius said. "I think your pater cannot see or hear me. Perhaps no-one in your time can see me."

"Come on. Get in the van," Mr. Page said, "We can't miss your appointment. I'll have to really put my foot down and the traffic's bad at this time of day."

Jack grabbed Julius and dragged him along the passage and out of the front door. He got into the front seat of the van next to his dad, pulling Julius in beside him and stretched across and slammed the door shut. It was a tight squeeze on the front bench seat for the three of them.

"Give us a bit of room, Son," his father said, assuming it was Jack's nervousness at having his plaster off, that made him sit so close. He revved up, noisily set the van in gear and headed for the hospital at top speed.

Julius squealed in absolute fear. His face was contorted and his eyes almost popped out of his head.

"It'll be alright," Jack said to console him.

"Of course it'll be alright" his father said, thinking Jack was talking to him. "You're not nervous about having the plaster off are you?"

"N..n..no," Jack stammered. "I was just telling Ju....."

"Oh it'll be fine," his dad said with a laugh. "Shall we get tea from that chippy again? That'll take your mind off it."

Jack understood that his father wasn't ignoring Julius. It was just that he couldn't actually see him but the situation was very odd. Julius meanwhile, had turned a very odd grey colour. Even the chariots in the races in Rome could not achieve this speed, he thought. He was convinced he was going to die. He felt the bile rising in the back of his throat.

"Please don't be sick Julius," Jack begged, "We're nearly

there now."

"Of course you're not going to be sick, Jack. It's nothing, having the plaster off. Nothing that a nice fish and chip supper won't cure."

Of course his father thought Jack was talking about himself. Julius risked a glance through the window. Monsters of all shapes and sizes sped past him on wheels. Others sped even faster towards them and he squeezed his eyes together and prayed inside his head that they wouldn't hurt him. They didn't. He noticed too, people buying merchandise at shops that were just a bit like those in his home town and he felt almost comforted. Eventually the thing they were in slowed and Julius sighed a sigh of relief.

"Go on, we've got to get out," Jack told him, "This is the hospital."

Mr. Page frowned. That was an odd thing, his son telling him to get out, but he let it drop.

It was Jack's turn to go an odd colour when he saw the technician coming towards him with a small electric saw and begin to slice through the plaster on his arm. What would happen if the man's hand slipped? He wondered. Julius was fascinated. Within a few minutes Jack's arm was free of the plaster and he was being quite cocky about having had it done. He wriggled his fingers about a bit and found his arm was back to normal strength.

"Next stop, fish and chip shop," his father said.

Thinking quickly, Jack told him,

"I could manage a big portion tonight Dad." At least he could share his tea with Julius even if his dad didn't know he was there.

Back in the van, Julius was beginning to enjoy himself. He was getting used to the movement and speed now and for the first time took a good look at the controls panel with all its dials and lights and flashing arrows. He watched intently over Jack's father's shoulder, as he turned the wheel and moved a large floor lever and pressed the pedals with his feet. The twenty-first century was proving to be exciting.

It was an odd meal. There were only two plates set out, Jack's with a huge pile of extra chips. They sat on armchairs round the TV and Jack shared his plateful with Julius. Mr. Page was so absorbed in the programme he didn't notice Jack's food going in two directions. Julius, hiding behind Jack's chair, shovelled in the fish and the strange potatoes called chips. He kept himself hidden from Jack's father. 'I might be invisible but the food may not be,' he thought. He wasn't really aware of eating. The moving picture box with its tiny people, bright colours and strange music, that Jack called a telly, quite took his breath away.

"Telly's good tonight," Jack said when his father left the room to answer the phone. Julius couldn't answer him. He just sat there with his mouth hanging open, watching the picture constantly changing. At one point he got up and stared into the back of the TV but he couldn't see how the people got inside.

"Wondrous!" he kept saying, "Wondrous!"

"Here, catch," Jack said, throwing him a can of coke. Julius watched what he did with the ring-pull and copied. He watched what he did next and copied. He took an enormous gulp from the can and spluttered as coke ran down his chin and on to his tunic.

"Go easy," Jack warned him. "It's fizzy!"

Before Jack's dad returned Julius made it clear he was anxious about getting home.

"Just going out for a bit, Dad," Jack called. His dad was

still on the phone. The boys headed for Two Tree Island.

They had just reached the start of the footbridge when Joss Smith and Zak Dreyfus leapt out at them from behind some bushes.

"See the plaster's gone. Yer fit to fight now then?"

Jack clutched his now un-plastered arm with the good one to protect it. They hadn't pushed him to the ground yet.

"Run for it Julius," he yelled, "These are the boys who hurt me. Get on to the island."

"He's gone bonkers!"

"Loopy more like!"

Zak and Josh were laughing at him. They hadn't even thumped him, just laughed. Jack looked at Julius in his tunic that still looked like a dress to him. Any minute now the atmosphere would blow. It was lucky they wouldn't be able to see Julius. Imagine what they'd make of a boy in a dress!

"Run for it!" he screamed at him again. It was a bit silly as they wouldn't actually see Julius but Jack wasn't taking any chances.

"Oh listen to 'im. He's got an imaginary friend. He won't help you!" yelled Josh, poking his finger hard and repeatedly into Jack's shoulder.

"You must not run away. We will stay and fight. You must fight like a centurion," advised Julius suddenly becoming dangerously brave. "You must be supreme and conquer your enemy."

Jack wasn't in a conquering mood but he tried. Arms flailing all over the place, he tried to hit out at the two bullies but they were stronger and out-manoeuvred him. They were enjoying themselves. It was great sport. They flicked at him again. At his face and his legs. At his head and his arms. All the time of course, not knowing he was there, they left Julius alone.

"Introduce us to your imaginary friend next time," Zak called sneeringly.

"That's the only kind of friend he'll ever get," called Josh as they started to run off.

Actually, Julius thought, it could be very useful that in twenty-first century Britain, he was invisible! Julius got close to the two boys as they ran by him. He stretched out and tweaked Josh's nose hard.

"Oy! Stop that Zak." Josh accused his friend of the attack. Julius tweaked even harder.

"Oy! Give it a rest!" Josh lashed out with his fist and caught Zak on his nose. It began to bleed.

"Gerroff! Stop it, stop it. I never touched yer!" Zak shrieked, wiping his nose on his cuff as his so-called friend appeared to be attacking him. "We're s'posed to be on the same side."

Jack stood, hands on his hips, screaming with laughter. He watched as Julius, enjoying the situation, pinched Zak's bottom.

"Ouch! And you can stop flipping laughing as well!"

The bullies now began to fight in earnest, pushing each other to the ground and grovelling in the dirt.

"That's brilliant Julius," Jack said between laughing hiccups.

The bullies stopped grappling and sheepishly moved off.

"We'll get you for this!" Zak threatened.

"We have to do something about the bullies." Jack sounded pretty hopeless.

"Yes. We must create a strategy," Julius agreed rather pompously. "We must stop them, the Britannian and the Roman bullies."

They both nodded in agreement then Jack said,

"But how?"

"Next time we meet," Julius replied, "We will make a way. But now I must return. My paterfamilias will worry."

"Oh Lord!" Jack's voice was full of panic. "How do we get you back? I came in and out with the coin. How did we get you in, I can't remember?"

"I was holding your magic," Julius said thoughtfully, "It is the only way."

Jack took his mobile phone out of his pocket and held it lovingly.

"I can't give you this," he said, shaking his head slowly. "Dad'll kill me."

But he knew it was the only way. Grudgingly he handed it to Julius.

"Hold it tight," he said quietly. "Please don't lose it."

Julius grasped the phone firmly. As he disappeared into nothingness, Jack yelled at the top of his voice,

"For God's sake don't lose it!"

CHAPTER 11

"Ben, can I ask you something?"

"Sure."

It was Sunday and Jack was at his Mum's, as usual at the weekend. She was getting a meal and Jack and Ben were in the sitting room. They had all spent the day at a brilliant theme park and Jack felt better about his stepfather. He had begun to trust him. Ben had been really nice to him. They had talked a lot and when they went for a swim at the local pool on the way back, Jack had almost let on about the bullying. Ben had noticed the bruises on his shoulder and arm where Zak and Josh had prodded him. In the end, although he'd hinted, Jack didn't actually mention bullying.

"What it is...well it's...." Jack was having difficulty getting to the point. He'd rather talk it over with Ben. His dad would only worry if he discussed it with him. Ben was separate, not so close.

"Ben, do you believe in time travel?"

Ben put on a serious face.

"What makes you ask that?"

Jack breathed deeply. He'd never imagined he'd ever tell anyone but it sort of seemed important now that at least somebody knew, in case...well in case something happened to him.

"It's just that......I've done it."

"Done what? You've done what?"

Was Ben being thick on purpose? He'd just told him the most important thing he'd ever told anyone and he was making out he didn't understand.

"It. Time travel. I've done it." Jack let the words out in a rush.

"Yeah? Sounds great." Ben was obviously humouring him. Jack could tell by the smirk on his face.

"Oh, it doesn't matter. It's nothing. It's not important." Jack shrugged and started to walk away.

"Wait a minute. I'm sorry. Tell me again," Ben said in that tone of voice adults use when they know they've said the wrong thing.

"Go on. I really want to know."

Jack wished he'd never started but it was too late so he blundered on.

"I've been to Roman Britain and seen stuff. My friend Julius showed me things. I went in his mum and dad's house...."

"Hold on, hold on. Not so fast. Are you sure you haven't been reading about this or something. I mean it's a great idea and it's great you've got such a vivid imagination. Your mother's good at writing stories you probably take after her and..."

"NO! NO! NO! It's not imagination. I have. Oh what's the use? I knew you wouldn't believe me!"

Jack stomped out of the room and breathlessly ran upstairs in a red-faced temper. He should never have said anything. Of course they wouldn't believe him. A thought occurred to him. He thudded downstairs again and burst into the living room, pushing the door back so hard it hit against the wall. His mum was in there too now.

"Anyway," he shouted angrily, "I've got the proof. Here.

Look at this."

He took the coin out of his pocket and held it out to them in his open palm and shouted at the top of his voice,

"This is a Roman coin. Julius told me. He's a Roman boy. He's my best friend. He wears a tunic and sandals. He's seen it work. If I'm in the right place and I hold this tightly, I can get in. I can! I can! I've been there. I've seen the blood on the weapons! I've, I've...."

"Come on Dear, don't get so upset." His mum put her arms round him. "We knew something was wrong. Is it that school? You can tell us. We'll sort it out. Just don't upset yourself. We hate to see you so unhappy."

How did he ever let this happen? If only he'd kept quiet. What was it with adults? They always got the wrong end of the stick and then they interfered all the time.

"This is the coin."

He wanted to explain but his brain wouldn't work. He watched as the two grown-ups looked at the coin. It looked just like any other old coin that might be dug up somewhere. Collectors searched for them with metal detectors on the beach at Leigh all the time. He absolutely knew this one was special but he watched their faces as they looked at it, forcing themselves to nod and smile politely. And watching their faces, he knew how pathetic he must have seemed. He took the coin back and put it in his pocket.

The evening meal was difficult, full of silences and half-hearted smiles. Just bits of conversation that were obviously avoiding the subject of time travel, the Romans and Jack's earlier outburst. Jack didn't eat very much even though his mum had done a roast. It was hard to swallow when you were feeling choked. He escaped up to his room as soon as he could.

After a while he heard raised voices from downstairs. His

mother said,

"It's no life for Jack. He's become a latch-key kid."

"It's not John's fault. He's got to earn a living." Ben was defending Jack's father.

"Well something's happened. He doesn't seem to have any proper friends. All he talks about is this imaginary boy Julius. If he's making up imaginary friends he's probably very lonely."

Jack was seething with anger. He wanted to tell them 'Julius isn't imaginary and he's the best friend I've ever had.' But what was the point? They wouldn't believe him. He listened in again as Ben spoke.

"When are we going to tell him we're moving to London?"

His mother's reply sent shivers down his spine.

"I want him to come with us, live with us in London. Let's give him a normal home life and I want to get him away from that school. Give him a fresh start."

Jack covered his ears. He couldn't bear to hear any more. He wouldn't go with them. He wouldn't. He wanted to stay with his dad. He wanted to be where he knew people even if he was bullied. He'd cope. He didn't want to go anywhere strange. And what about Julius? London was fifty miles away from Two Tree Island. How on earth would he get to see Julius then?

Jack felt sick. He wished he could see Julius right now. He wished he could speak to him. Julius still had Jack's mobile. If only he'd shown him how to read text messages he could have borrowed another mobile and texted him. If only.....

At that precise moment, the moment when his mind was on Julius, Jack could have sworn he heard his mobile ring. Without thinking he put his hand in his pocket to answer the phone. But of course, his phone wasn't there. What he pulled out of his pocket was the coin.

"I've got to get to the island," he thought. "I've got to get there now!" He didn't know why it was so urgent. It just was.

His mum and Ben were still deep in conversation. Jack crept downstairs and made for the front door. Unseen and unheard he escaped up the front path and began running. His mother's house was three times further from the island than his own but breathless and sweating despite the chill night, he sprinted towards Two Tree in pitch blackness.

On two Tree Island in Roman Britain, Julius had temporarily forgotten about the three bullies who had been making his life a misery. He was with his paterfamilias on a trip to the circus.

A huge circular area had been prepared and named 'The Circus Minimus' because it was so much smaller than 'The Circus Maximus' in Rome. It had rows and rows of stone seating round the circle, rising in tier after tier. In this way, everyone had a good view of the floor of the circus, the circus ring. There were four teams, reds, blues, greens and whites competing in amazing chariot races. Julius and his father supported the greens and Julius had watched as his paterfamilias had pledged money on the winner. Twelve chariots ran in each race, pulled sometimes by two, sometimes three and sometimes four huge horses.

As the whip-wielding charioteers stood and guided the horses so the chariots didn't tip over, Julius got caught up in the excitement of the yelling, cheering masses of men watching. He leapt up on to the tiered, stone seating to get a better view and joined in with the men shouting for their favourite to win.

As the charioteers raced their chariots harder and harder round the seven laps of the circus, the crowd grew wilder and wilder with excitement. In the last race the speed of the chariots was so great that one huge chariot pulled by four great steeds took the bend too fast on the third lap and it crashed to the ground. It crushed the charioteer, freeing the four frightened horses to gallop off in all different directions. But the chariot was one of the red team so it didn't stop Julius and his father and the rest of the green team supporters yelling and screaming for their team to win.

"YAHH!" The shout went up. The greens had won. Julius knew what to do. As the crowd of men jostled to collect their winnings, cheering and shouting, he knew he must sit and wait while his father collected their money and then came back for him. On the way home they would stop in the market and buy a trinket for his mother.

The crowd dispersed and Julius sat alone on the stone tier and waited for his father. The sun was hot, beating down on his head and neck, and he was pleased to be seated under the velarium, a great awning that shaded the audience from the heat of the sun.

Julius lay back against the tier behind and just let his eyes close for a moment. He could hear the swishing of water. The officials had waited until the arena was clear and now they were filling the centre of the circus with water. When it was deep enough and the audience had returned to the upper levels there were to be mock sea battles for everyone to watch.

"WAAA!" A terrific scream blasted into Julius's ears and before he could catch his breath hands grabbed him, pushing and shoving him downwards to the bottom of the stone tiers. The swishing of the water grew louder and louder and more ferocious as Julius was shoved nearer and nearer the bottom towards the fast filling arena.

Catching his breath he managed to get a glance at his attackers. He might have guessed. Their green boy soldier uniforms easily picking them out, the three bullies, Brutus, Augustus and Flavius had chosen this moment to attack him when all the adults had filed out and Julius was temporarily alone.

Now Julius could feel the ice-cold water splashing on his legs and his tunic but still the boys pushed him forward. He never imagined that water could sound so loud.

"Help me! Help me!" he cried but his shouts were feeble and drowned out by the swirling, thundering water and the wicked, excited whoops of the boys.

Suddenly the three hooligans lifted Julius high off the ground and chucked him headlong into fast-moving water.

Gasping for air, glugging, choking, half-blinded, something made Julius struggle to get his hand in his pocket and extract Jack's mobile phone.

"For God's sake don't lose it!" The last words Jack had said to him came back to Julius in a rush. Never mind that he was going to drown. The only thing he could think of was to get Jack's magic to safety.

Struggling hopelessly against the force of the water, he finally managed to grab the magic and splashing with his feet, keep afloat while he held it above the water. Each time he surfaced he caught the wicked laughter of the three bullies.

Tighter and tighter he held the mobile, gasping for breath, kicking his legs, his head ducking under the water and still he grasped the precious magic so tightly he was almost squeezing it in half.

"Julius! Julius! I'm here! I'm coming!"

Suddenly there was Jack's voice, faint at first then stronger and stronger.

"Jack? Is that you? When did you get here?" Julius's voice was weak. He was soaked and exhausted but his great friend

Jack had returned to Roman times to rescue him.

"No Julius. I'm not there. You're here with me. You're in the twenty-first century. You've come back. I knew. I felt it. I knew you needed me."

Weakly Julius looked around in the dark and strained his eyes to see. Realising with relief, that he was once more in the twenty-first century and out of danger from drowning in the arena, his knees buckled and he sank to the ground.

"It was the magic," he gasped faintly. "I was saving the magic from danger. I held it so tightly it got me here."

CHAPTER 12

"Jack, I cannot return to Roman times. I am vanquished. The bullies have won. They tried to drown me in the arena. I shall never see Rome again!"

As he hiccoughed back the tears, a shivering, dripping, frightened Julius, his teeth chattering constantly, stutteringly told Jack what had happened, finishing with the words,

"I am disgraced and I have run away to the future! Here, I must stay."

Jack gave Julius a look of horror.

"Don't be daft. How can you stay here? No-one can see you except me. You're invisible. You're soaking wet and I can't even lend you some of my clothes."

"I would owe you much gratitude for some dry clothes. My tunic is heavy with water and I have wondered often since I met you how it would be to wear trousers."

Jack noticed Julius sounded really old-fashioned and even more Roman than last time. He hadn't been so aware of his odd language when they last met. He shook his head.

"My clothes CAN be seen," he said, "But your body can't. Just think what would happen if someone saw you. My trousers would be floating around all by themselves!...."

At that thought both boys laughed hysterically but Julius knew Jack was right.

"Anyway," Jack continued, "What happened to your 'I will

be a centurion. I will win the fight, soldiers don't run away attitude?' You've changed your tune a bit haven't you?"

Julius stared back at him slowly shaking his head.

"I was mistaken. I am not brave enough. I would be a bad soldier. I would disgrace my paterfamilias."

As Julius stood there looking small and insignificant, a pool of water had collected round his feet where his tunic had dripped. It was dark and shafts of street light reflected in the puddle, shimmering as the wind ruffled its surface.

"Come on," Jack instructed grabbing his friend's arm and pulling him forwards, "We've got to get you sorted out and I think I've got a great idea."

The boys began to run, Jack picking up speed and Julius, weak as he was, trying hard to keep up. As they ran, Julius felt the mobile vibrating in his hand.

"Jack, Jack, the magic is moving!" he shrieked.

Still keeping up the pace, Jack glanced at the display screen. His mother was texting him, asking where he was and if he was all right. He decided to ignore the message but told Julius about dashing out of his mum's house without telling her.

"We haven't got much time because they'll expect me back," he said, "Just let's go to my home, my dad's house. I need something, then I'll tell you what my idea is."

It was well into the March evening now, so in cover of darkness they crept up the path to Jack's house. His father's van was not on the driveway. That meant Dad was out on a job and running late or maybe he had gone to the supermarket, which he did after work usually.

"Come on. Let's hope Dad doesn't get back yet. He'll want to know why I'm not at Mum's." Jack whispered just in case, "Follow me."

He led Julius upstairs to his bedroom and began rummaging

in his cupboard. Julius just kept touching things. He eyed the TV that Jack's dad had given him for his last Christmas present.

"You have another magic like the big one downstairs," Julius said, touching it warily. "Make it work, make it work." He was shouting now, excited by the prospect of what this magic box might do.

It was on stand-by so Jack used the remote.

"More magic, more magic. It works without you touching it. I shall stay here for ever in this world of marvels." Julius was red in the face with excitement now and couldn't take his eyes off the action on the TV screen.

"Come on, I've got what I've been looking for."

Jack was getting exasperated as Julius seemed unaware of the urgency. Jack didn't want his dad to come back and find him there. He'd ask all sorts of questions about why he'd come home from his mum's and why he hadn't told anyone. And more specifically, why he hadn't used his mobile to let him know what was happening.

He made one last effort at dragging Julius out of the room.

"I've got something that will help to cure your bullies," he told him but Julius wanted to stay in twenty-first century Britain. It had a lot more to offer than the Roman one.

"What are these buttons?" he asked, fingering Jack's computer keyboard as if it was a piano.

"Stop!" yelled Jack, "It's on stand-by. You'll lose everything. Oh Lord! That history essay was my homework. It took me hours. I'll so be dead tomorrow! My teacher goes crazy if you don't get work in on time!"

Jack eyed the screen as his thousand word essay scrolled down deleting words at speed, lost for ever in some irretrievable part of the computer's memory. He let out a huge sigh.

"Let's get going," he said

They were halfway down the stairs when they heard the key in the lock. Jack froze. Julius continued leaping downstairs, whistling the tune from Coronation Street that he'd picked up from ogling Jack's TV.

"Jack, is that you? What are you doing home? Is everything all right?"

Jack prayed his dad hadn't heard Julius whistling.

"Yeah Dad, fine. I just needed something. I'm going back to Mum's now."

Julius was still invisible and silent to other people. Jack sighed with relief. He needn't have worried. Dad was far too preoccupied with a guest but he seemed embarrassed to find Jack at home. A quite nice woman with red hair, about his father's age, had walked in the door behind him.

"Jack, this is Stacy. She works at the supermarket. We often have a chat. She's come back to borrow that book I got on Roman Pottery. Her hobby's archaeology."

His dad's words came out in a terrible rush. Jack let a smile hover on his lips as he said 'hi' to her then he asked his dad,

"Is she your girl-friend Dad?"

His father spluttered a bit, then said,

"Would you mind if she was?"

"Nah, it's fine."

Jack was pushing the unseen Julius out of the front door now.

"See yer Dad. 'Bye Stacy,"

Once they were out of earshot Jack said,

"I had planned to go back to Two Tree but now Dad's seen me, I'll have to go to Mum's."

Julius frowned.

"And me? What about me? I cannot survive in your world

without you."

"You can come with me of course. Just be careful not to move anything or make them suspicious. You can bunk down in my room. OK?"

"Bunk down? What is Bunk down? It does not sound nice." It was beginning to dawn on Julius that things were a lot more complicated than he had realized.

"It just means go to sleep for the night. If they can't see you or hear you, everything will be OK. It's just if you move anything and they see, we'll get sussed."

Julius shook his head. More strange words, but what was he to do? In this century he'd just have to do whatever Jack told him to. He began to understand why Jack had been so frightened in Roman times.

They raced up his mum's front path and Jack rang the doorbell. His mother opened the door in a panic.

"Where on earth have you been at this time of night? I was just about to phone your father."

"Sorry," Jack said lightly, "I needed something."

He belted upstairs dragging Julius behind him, and headed for his room.

"As long as you're not upset about us moving…." His mother's voice followed him but he was concentrating on his idea and didn't reply.

As they settled down for the night the boys spoke in whispers. Jack said,

"You know what? I've got to go to school tomorrow. Looks like you'll have to come too."

"I feel great terror at that thought," Julius replied honestly. "Can we not go immediately to the place you call Two Tree?"

"Nah!" Jack said," I daren't bunk off school. They'd all be suspicious and come looking for me. That really would spell disaster."

Breakfast the next morning was a bit like a pantomime. Jack ate his cereal slowly and when his mother and stepfather weren't looking, shovelled pieces of buttered toast and crispy rashers of bacon into his pockets.

"Don't eat your bacon before your cereal," his mother said, "You'll be sick."

"Can I have some more bacon?" Jack asked. He'd been so busy stashing away food for Julius, he hadn't eaten any himself.

"My goodness you're hungry this morning," his mother replied. She passed him another couple of rashers. "Is your father feeding you properly?"

Jack was too busy eating to reply.

All this time, Julius had been standing by the door, partly to keep out of the way and partly to be ready to make a dash for it if he suddenly became visible. He was intrigued to watch the rituals of the morning in a twenty-first century home. He tried to commit to memory everything he saw. When he returned, if he returned to his own time, he would like to tell someone about it all. But who would believe him?

The journey to school was magic. In the back of the car, sitting behind his mum and Ben, Jack couldn't stop giggling. What would they say if they knew Jack was not alone in the back? That his companion was Roman. And from hundreds of years ago at that? He thrust his hand into his pocket and withdrew a soggy piece of toast and two bedraggled and fluffy rashers of bacon.

"Here, have this," he whispered, "But eat quietly."

"What did you say, Dear?" his mother asked.

"Nothing."

"But I heard you...."

"First sign of madness, talking to yourself," Ben joined in.

Jack started giggling again, especially when he noticed a huge wodge of pocket fluff curling from Julius's bottom lip. After they were dropped off at the school gate, Jack said,

"Just keep close to me and don't do anything odd. You know what I mean. You can sit on the floor near my desk each lesson but for God's sake don't get in the way so someone falls over you or all hell'll be let loose."

Julius nodded.

"Ready then?" Jack asked.

"He's only talking to himself again, the nutter."

"You mean her little Einstein."

It was the bullies, Josh and Zak. They twisted their forefingers to their heads to show they thought Jack was mad.

"We'll get you later," they threatened, as the school bell went.

"I recognise your bullies." Julius said. How could he forget them?

"Yeah! Don't be fooled into thinking they're OK. 'cause they are truly wicked. And I mean in the Roman sense. Cruel. Nasty. Awful. They've made my life real hell."

Julius said no more. He could tell by Jack's reaction that those two were just like the three who'd attacked him back home in Roman Britain.

Julius settled himself on the floor, leaning against Jack's desk. It was history. Mrs. Hunter was returning books in her usual fashion. Julius laughed aloud as she sent them flying across the room like a Roman discus thrower.

Julius watched as the lesson progressed. He could see who were the pupils who did not concentrate. He could see that his friend Jack was clever. He could feel the atmosphere of nastiness that was aiming towards Jack from the back row where Josh and Zak and a couple of their gang were laughing and behaving badly. They were writing nasty notes, pointing at Jack and all the time only doing all this when the teacher's back was turned.

Julius had an idea. Carefully he crept to the back of the room making sure not to brush against anything or anyone. He slithered down on to the floor between Zak and Josh's desks. When Zak had turned to hand a nasty note forwards so that it got handed down to Jack's desk, Julius struck. He lifted Zak's history book and threw it as hard as he could at Mrs. Hunter so that it hit her full pelt in the middle of her back. She spun round from the board.

"You little brats!" she yelled. "Who threw that?"

Silence. No-one owned up.

"Well that's easily solved." She used a threatening voice and turning the book over, read the name on the front cover.

"Zak Dreyfus, get out of my classroom," she screamed.

"But I never. It wasn't me. I didn't do...."

"OUT!" She pointed to the door.

Zak shuffled out of the room in the certain knowledge that for once he was telling the truth.

"'Snot fair," he muttered as he left the room.

Next, Julius stooped carefully forward and grabbing a huge handful of hair from the girl who sat in front of Josh, pulled with all his might.

"OWWWW!" Chelsea Jones exploded into a massive scream of pain.

"Miss, Miss," she sobbed, "Josh Smith's blooming scalped me."

Mrs. Hunter had had enough. As she stormed up the gangway between the desks, Julius leapt out of the way just in time. She grabbed Josh by the collar of his scruffy shirt and hauled him to the door.

"Get out, get out," she barked. "Get yourself, on report mind you, to the headmaster and don't come back this week."

"But I-I-I never," Josh stammered. It was no good. Mrs. Hunter had spoken.

The lesson continued relatively peacefully. When the teacher had gone and the other kids had filed out, Jack lingered.

"Was that you, all that stuff?"

Julius couldn't help laughing as he admitted that it was.

They managed to get through the day without anyone suspecting anything. At home time they returned to Jack's dad's house. There was a note on the kitchen table.

Dear Jack,

Am meeting Stacy after work. Help yourself to supper. It's in the oven on the pre-timer and should be ready by 5.30. Ring me if you need me. Afterwards go round and stay the night at your Mum's as I don't want you on your own all evening. See you later. Love Dad.

"Well that's made things easy," Jack said. "We can share it then we'll go to Two Tree."

After they had eaten Jack urged,

"Come on. Let's get down to Two Tree now. We're 'going Roman' and I've got something that'll sort out your bullies."

It was dark. Jack reckoned even if he was missed and his mum and Ben came looking for him in the car, they wouldn't see him. The boys slowed their pace a little but kept walking. It was eerie down by Leigh train station as they began to walk across the bridge towards Two Tree Island, so Jack kept on talking to Julius. It was a defence mechanism against the frightening shadows and weird sounds that come with the night.

"What it is," Jack started to explain his idea to a not very interested Julius, "If you can be bothered to listen, is I've got my dad's old instamatic camera..."

But he didn't get any further.

"Well just look who it is!"

The disembodied sarcastic voice loomed out of the shadows. Zak Dreyfus with Josh Smith following behind.

Jack caught his breath.

"How did you know I was here?" he asked nervously, backing up against the wall of the bridge.

"We know everything about you. We know where you are at all times."

"We can get you whenever we want!"

The two boys, wicked intent in their eyes, edged forward towards Jack, bearing down on him, enjoying the sport of seeing him afraid. They sneered. They poked at him. To Jack they seemed to tower over him although in reality they weren't much taller than he was.

Shaking with fear he slithered to the ground against the bridge wall as the two bullies began swiping his legs with sticks, hitting his face and arms and chest.

"Run for help Julius, get someone, ring the police!" he managed to scream but even as he uttered the words he knew all those things were impossible. Julius was Roman and invisible. He couldn't.

"Oh sweet! The mad boy's talking to his pretend friend again. Think he's going to save you, do you?"

"Huh! Think again!"

"Get away from Jack. Get away from my friend!" Yelled Julius. But he couldn't be heard. *He needs me. I must help him,* he thought. *But how?*

The two attackers now had their arms raised, about to really beat the living daylights out of Jack, who was a whimpering heap on the ground at their feet. He braced himself for the next onslaught.

Maybe it was the nasty snigger in their voices, maybe the fear that they would really harm his friend or maybe just the memory of what his own bullies had put him through that forced a huge strength into Julius. He grasped hold of some broken bricks that had crumbled from the base of the old bridge.

He placed his feet and body in the stance as he had been taught for discus throwing, to get the best shot with the greatest force, and he let fly. The first piece caught Josh right in the stomach. He let out a desperate howl and fell to the ground clutching his gut.

The second and third, following up fast, smashed against Zak's ankles knocking him off his feet. The aim was spot on. Jack was still on the ground, his eyes wide as saucers as the two bullies, screaming in pain, crying, panting with fear, scrambled to their feet and began to hobble away.

"How did you do that? We'll tell! We'll report you. You're a bully! We'll go to the police and tell them you hurt us," they yelled pathetically.

Once again, thanks to Julius, the tables turned on them. Josh and Zak limped away. They constantly turned back to threaten Jack, who was now lying on the ground guffawing with uncontrollable laughter despite his bruised body. Julius was so happy he flung his arms in the air in excitement, Jack's mobile phone still clutched in his non-throwing hand.

The street lamps on the bridge had now come on brightly, lighting up the spot where Julius and Jack were. Josh and Zak's lasting memory of that evening was a mobile phone, its VDU lit up, dancing up and down in the air by itself like a ghostly yoyo.

Jack and Julius took a few minutes to get their breath back but were so thrilled by their victory that they were ready for anything.

"Hold the mobile tightly and stand close by me," Jack instructed him. He himself clutched the Roman coin in one hand and his father's instamatic camera in the other.

CHAPTER 13

At 7am. in Leigh-on-Sea, a phone rang.

"John, is that you? Has Jack come home yet?"

"No!"

"John, we've been out all night looking for him. The police have too. I'm terribly worried. So's Ben."

Jack's mother was far more than worried but was trying to keep her voice calm so as not to upset her ex-husband any more than was necessary.

Mr. Page was puzzled.

"He seemed alright yesterday. He just popped back here to pick something up and then he headed back to your place. Come to think about it he did seem a bit on edge. Anxious to get going. Didn't say anything though."

"He didn't come back here. Did he talk about this imaginary friend of his then?"

Mr. Page frowned.

"What imaginary friend? That's ridiculous. Jack's a sensible lad. He wouldn't have......."

"But he has. He did. He's been saying odd things, to Ben not to me. They had a heart to heart and...."

Mr. Page interrupted.

"I'll get the van out and go and have a look. I think he's got interested in bird-watching. He's been spending time down on Two Tree Island recently, at the bird sanctuary I suppose.

Tried to tell me there was a film crew down there but that's nonsense. And staying out all night is just NOT acceptable behaviour."

Jack's mother breathed in deeply.

"John, I think he's run away. I think it might be our fault."

John Page could tell, even over the phone that Jack's mother was crying.

"How do you mean, your fault?"

"Ben and I are going to go and live in London. We want Jack to come with us. It's no life for a lad coming home to an empty house."

"Did you tell Jack about this idea?" Jack's father asked.

"Yes. He heard us talking about it I think."

"And?"

"He obviously didn't like the thought of leaving you or the school or...... but we only said it for the best. I really think he's run away because of us."

Mr. Page knew his son better than most. He was sure he wouldn't do anything silly. Of course, he had broken his arm recently and they'd never really got to the bottom of that. And if he really thought about it, he had heard Jack talking to himself once or twice. And he never seemed to use his mobile phone much. Now that wasn't normal in a lad his age. Everywhere he went, Mr. Page saw kids with a phone practically attached to one ear, but not Jack. Perhaps there was something up. He spoke to Jack's mother again.

"Look, the first thing is to find him, make sure he's OK. Then I can put his and your mind at rest. He won't be coming home to an empty house much longer. I've met someone. Stacy. We're getting married and before you say anything, yes, Jack's met her and they got on alright."

They finished their conversation on a good note. Jack would

have a normal home life from now on and his mother and Ben could move to London without having to worry about him.

There was only one problem. First of all, they'd have to find Jack.

At 8.am on that day, Mr. Harris, the head-teacher of Jack's school, sat in the staffroom and, with a very worried look on his face, watched until all the teachers and other members of staff had squeezed into every available space.

"Thank you all for getting here so early to attend this special meeting," he said sombrely. "I have some very worrying news to tell you."

A murmur went round the room as people wondered what might be wrong. Mr. Harris continued,

"One of our year seven boys has gone missing. His father phoned me this morning and the police have been called in."

"Which one?"

"Who is it?"

"What can have happened?" Everyone started talking at the same time. Mr. Harris held up his hand for quiet.

"The boy's name is Jack Page."

For a few seconds there was a stunned silence.

"Jack's one of the nicest boys I've ever taught," said one teacher.

"He's my brightest," said Mrs. Hunter. A few others, including one of the dinner ladies, made similar comments. Then another teacher spoke.

"I had a word with Jack the other day. I think someone has been having a go at him, been bullying him or something. I gave him a chance to tell me but he wouldn't say anything. Just looked scared and went off to class. Of course, he does have a broken arm at the moment."

"Talking of bullying," said the games master, "I've been

planning to say something at the next staff meeting. We've got a problem in year seven and we need to put a stop to it."

Another teacher joined in.

"I've had to tell a couple of boys off more than once for…."
He was interrupted by one of the female teachers.

"It's not just boys. There's bullying among the girls too!"
Mr. Harris looked shocked.

"Well, are you suggesting that Jack has been hurt by bullies? Or has run away because of them? Whatever happens, we must sort this out here and now!"

It was very nearly time for school to start and the bell was about to ring, before the meeting reached its conclusion. Ten of the teachers in the room had jotted down a vast list of notes showing what they had seen, who they had told off, who they had put in detention for bad behaviour and a lot of other stuff, since the beginning of the term.

Mr. Harris thought about what he had been told during the past three quarters of an hour. He studied the notes in his hand before asking in a menacingly quiet voice,

"And we are all agreed who the main culprits are?" In one loud voice, the teachers replied,

"Josh Smith and Zak Dreyfus!"

At 11am on the same day, the school secretary showed two sets of parents into the head-teacher's office.

"Mr. and Mrs. Smith, Mr. and Mrs. Dreyfus, please do come in and sit down."

Broderick Harris had been head-teacher of the comp. for over twenty-years. He'd seen it all. Clever kids, thick kids, troublesome ones, helpful ones. Kids he could cope with, without turning a hair. But parents! Parents were the bane of his life. Schools would be far better places if parents were banned. Full stop. He pushed his glasses back up his nose and opened the top file on his desk, skimmed it for a moment or two then did the same with the file underneath.

The two sets of parents shuffled uncomfortably on their chairs, especially Shane Dreyfus, Zak Dreyfus' father, a thick-necked, muscular man obviously champing at the bit and angry.

The headmaster pushed his glasses down again and looked over the top of them at his visitors.

"Now," he said "How may I help you?"

"We want him expelled."

"He needs a good thrashing."

"He didn't half hurt my poor Zak."

"We're thinking of taking out a summons."

All four parents started shouting at once.

"One at a time Ladies and Gentlemen if you please!" shouted Mr. Harris in a typically headmaster's voice, "And exactly who is it that you want expelled?"

"Jack Page!" they all shouted at once.

"He's a thug!" Mrs. Dreyfus added with a snarl.

Broderick Harris frowned, coughed and looked again at the files on his desk.

"Amazing," he commented, "Utterly so! He's such a quiet insignificant boy. Quite polite. Hard-working too."

Zak's father, Shane Dreyfus, stood up, hunched his shoulders and looked menacingly at the headmaster.

"Right, well are you going to get on with it or are we going to have to get nasty? Mmm?"

Mr. Harris remained quite calm.

"Sit down please," he said with the voice of authority, "And I will tell you."

Over the top of his glasses he gave the four visitors a withering look then referring to the files again, he began.

"The boy to whom you are referring is currently missing from home. The police have been called in."

At the word 'police' Shane Dreyfus shifted uncomfortably in his chair. He didn't like the cops. The head continued.

"We rather suspect that young Jack Page is missing because he has been on the receiving end and NOT the giving end of bullying. My sports teacher has observed certain things that he has recently made me aware of. In fact if Jack had been in school today, I had intended questioning him about a broken arm, HIS broken arm and how he came to break it."

This time Josh Smith's mother spoke.

"My boy arrived home frightened for his life. He was in such a state. Ghosts and magic he was talking about. Mobile phones that moved through the air with nobody holding them. Hysterical he was....and bruised. Couldn't speak proper, he was so scared. All he managed to get out was the boy's name. Jack Page. That's all he managed."

The other three parents muttered agreement.

Broderick Harris swivelled the folders round so they faced towards his visitors.

"Read these," he commanded.

As Josh and Zak's parents began to read the contents of the files, their faces turned red, then white then finally a weirdly angry purple.

"Never!" they yelled.

"Not our boys!"

"Rubbish!"

They refused to believe the words that stared up at them from the Headmaster's files. While Jack had been too scared to tell the teachers about the bullying, other boys had not. Jack had not been the only one to suffer at their hands and so many children and parents had complained that the teachers had also been watching Zak and Josh very closely, especially the sports staff. Page after page listed all the bullying and taunting and nasty deeds the boys had got up to. There were dates and times and even a letter from one kid's doctor stating he had seen the bruises.

Mr. Harris waited a few moments until the truth finally dawned on the four adults in his room, that their sons were bullies of the worst kind and that they had been found out.

Mr. Harris cleared his throat before saying in a most solemn tone of voice,

"In the event, I am sure you will understand why I must ask you to withdraw your boys from the school. Indeed with that kind of behaviour they are no longer welcome here!"

Mr. and Mrs. Dreyfus and Mr. and Mrs. Smith got slowly to their feet. They kept their eyes focussed on the ground. They didn't dare look the Headmaster or each other in the eye. They were ashamed. They shuffled to the door heads hung low. Mr. Dreyfus was the last to leave. Suddenly he turned to Mr. Harris and shouted,

"The little blighter. I'll have his guts for garters!" It was his son that he was talking about. And as an afterthought he added,

"I don't know where he gets it from!"

CHAPTER 14

In the Roman settlement on Two Tree Island, it was morning and the weather was bright. Jack and Julius had arrived for a purpose. They made their way towards the fort, part of which had been allocated as a boy soldiers' training college. Keeping close to the huge walls that surrounded the place they were able to stay in the shadows and silently move along unnoticed.

Discovering that security was less since their last visit, Julius pointed out that the gate at the college end of the fort was wide-open. He squeezed his body flat against the wall only allowing his head to overlap the sturdy gatepost as he peered around it to see what was happening.

Groups of boys in the green uniform of trainee soldiers were practising skills. Two groups were marching in battle formation, turning to the left or the right or fully about, as the huge officer in charge barked his orders. Other groups of boys were practising with blunted weapons, spears, swords or daggers, leaping this way and that and all responding without question, to the orders of the huge men in charge.

Julius beckoned to Jack to come closer and take a look for himself, then he whispered to him,

"It is difficult to pick out which of them is Brutus, Augustus or Flavius. They all look alike in their uniforms. We will have to wait here until they are free to walk outside the fort."

The two boys sat down on the grassy slope, close to the wall and waited. Jack put the coin safely in his pocket and then checked out his Dad's old instamatic camera, the sort that printed instant pictures, to make sure it was ready to use. They sat there for a long time, waiting, waiting, waiting.

Suddenly they were alerted to the drone and babble of boys' voices nearing the gate. Their morning free time had arrived.

"Are you ready?" Julius whispered to Jack. Jack nodded and stood back a little way. A stream of boys rushed and tumbled, walked or ran noisily through the gate. At last Julius recognised the boys he was waiting for. He stood and moved forward to bar their way.

"Salutations," he called brightly as if the three were his friends.

"Hail to the boy soldiers."

Now his voice was sarcastic. He needed to make the boys angry. He knew he must be brave and do this but inside he was shaking with fright. He knew the wicked things they could do to him but he told himself that if he was to truly be a fine centurion, then he must overcome his fear.

The three Roman bullies, realising who was making fun of them, began sneering.

"It is the cheat."

"It is the doctor's son, too lily-livered to be a proper soldier, who gets his pater to forge his soldier documents."

"It is the fool we drowned. Why is he not dead, drowned by the dribbling water of a pool?"

And they began to push him, first this way, then that. To prod and poke at him and slap his face. Julius stood his ground. This time they would not get the better of him.

"Stop!" he shouted. "I have magic to show you."

The three boys stopped dead, rooted to the ground in surprise and before they could say anything, Julius commanded in a voice louder than he had ever used before,

"Stand close together in a line."

Brutus, Augustus and Flavius were flabbergasted to hear Julius use a voice of such strength. These boys had spent days being drilled as soldiers. They were now accustomed to following orders. To obeying the voice of authority. They did as he instructed.

Julius put his arms out behind him as Jack, unseen by the soldier cadets, put the camera in his hand. Julius turned it towards the three bullies and clicked the button as Jack had instructed him. After a few moments, a photo slid out of the front of the camera. Julius, holding it carefully by a corner, pulled it free from the camera casing and waved it about to dry.

The three boys weren't sure what to do. Julius looked at the photo and laughed then seeing the bullies appear unsure and frightened, suddenly felt empowered. He took a bold step towards them.

"See this," he shouted, "Your images. Your exact images. Look!"

He flourished the photograph at them. The three Roman boys gasped at what they saw. As they stared at the magic that Julius held out, they were staring at themselves. Their own images stared back at them.

"I had no wish to do this but you left me no choice." Julius' voice was strangely grown up. He held tight to the photograph and continued,

"Note that you are my captives now and for all time!" The bullies staggered back, scared stiff. They dropped to the ground before Julius, frightened at what they had done. They had hurt a man of magic, had tried to drown him, to kill him.

They would be doomed forever.

Grovelling on the ground they began to whine,

"Forgive us Sir, for our sins."

"Show mercy mighty Julius, we recognise you are great with magic unknown."

Flavius said nothing. Scared witless, he just blubbered and dribbled like a baby. Julius held his head high. Now he would join the soldier school in his own right and everyone would know he was not a coward. He WOULD become a centurion. As his tormentors scuttled away he turned to Jack,

"Thank you my friend. You have made my future possible. I shall never forget you. Now I must go but first I must return your magic to you."

Something made Jack shiver. Julius handed the mobile phone and the camera to him and as their fingers touched, Jack could hardly see him. Julius had begun to fade.

"Pax vobis, Jack. Peace to you," he said and even his voice had become weak.

"Julius, Julius, you can't go, not now!"

But it was too late. Jack was startled by the weight of a hand on his shoulder.

"Hello young man. And where have you been?"

Jack looked up to where the voice had come from, frowning as he saw a uniformed policeman. A twenty-first century policeman. For a moment he was totally disorientated. The policeman spoke again in a gentle, kindly voice,

"You OK mate? Your mum and dad have been looking for you all night. You didn't half get them worried."

Jack stared around. Once again it was early morning. There were cars and the sound of an aeroplane. A bus chugged up the hill in the distance, over in Leigh. A train rumbled past towards the station. Two Tree Island was normal. The fort had gone and so had Julius. Jack hadn't meant to come back yet. He hadn't said 'goodbye' properly. For a split second he thought about holding the coin and getting back to Julius but at that moment his father, closely followed by his mum and Ben, came running towards him, arms outstretched.

"Thank God you're safe," they cried, and "Where have you been, why didn't you ring?" and then his mother said,

"Jack it's all right. You don't have to come to London with us. Please don't run away again. You can stay with your father. Everything will be fine. Even school now."

The grown-ups were all talking at once and Jack really couldn't make sense of what they were saying especially about school. Then he heard his father say to the policeman,

"Thank you, Officer, we'll take over now." Then to Jack he said,

"Why didn't you tell us you were being bullied?"

Jack couldn't take it all in. His father explained that the head-master had contacted him. They had had a meeting with all the parents of bullied boys and girls and assured them it wouldn't happen again as the ring-leaders had been expelled. Jack smiled. Actually it was quite good to be home here in twenty-first century Leigh-on-Sea. Suddenly he felt terribly, terribly hungry.

"Dad, can we go and get a burger, I'm starving?"

They all did. Jack and his father. Jack's mum and Ben and even Jack's dad's new girl-friend Stacey, whom Jack thought was rather nice.

It was when they had all eaten so much that they couldn't manage another mouthful that Stacey said something that took Jack's breath away.

"It's interesting that you go to Two Tree Island so often Jack," she began, "Is it an interest in the bird sanctuary like your dad says or is it for the archaeology?"

Jack frowned and just shook his head as she continued,

"Only you know I'm interested in archaeology and they've been doing a dig there at the far end of the island, some professors from London are involved. They've found quite a few artifacts, all Roman of course."

At the word 'Roman' Jack became alert. She went on,

"Apparently there was a Roman settlement there and they've found eating vessels and a small part of a mosaic floor and a few other things. Oh yes, and evidence of a soldier school and a bit of a tombstone of the man they think ran the school. Yes, here it is." At that point she brought out a copy of the local paper, The Leigh Herald.

"Look," she said folding the page back to show Jack the article and the photograph of the tombstone.

Jack looked at the picture and the words beneath. The inscription carved into the jagged piece of stone in a foreign script, was barely visible. Beneath the picture was printed the English translation.

'JULIUS VALENS, GREAT SOLDIER AND GOVERNOR OF BOHAZ COLLEGIATE.'

As he read the words, Jack clasped the coin that was in his pocket. His special Roman coin. There were things that he knew and he knew that they were fact. Real factual happenings and the knowledge was his and his alone. He could never tell anyone about Julius. It was his personal, private secret.

He smiled a secretive smile. Barely audibly, so that nobody else could hear, Jack whispered,

"Pax vobis, Julius!"